CASTING THE STONES

Speaker shook the stones inside the leather pouch, then upended the bag. There was a shower of stones, a number of them falling inside the circle the seer had drawn. He leaned forward to study the circle. Suddenly his body grew still. Speaker turned to look at Hawk.

"What is it?" asked Hawk, his mouth suddenly dry.

Although he leaned forward and stared at the stones himself, he could make no reason of what he saw.

"Two men," said Speaker, after a long moment's hesitation. "Two men will arrive from the south." He held up each stone as he spoke of it so that Hawk might understand. "You see here; two stones, both men, here in the bottom of the circle. Here in the center, this stone is the village. One of the men has a short leg or has suffered a leg injury."

Speaker held up the spear point. "They do not come with peace in their hearts," he said. "They come for blood. They come for you."

BROTHER
TO THE
LION

Rose Estes

BANTAM BOOKS
TORONTO • NEW YORK • LONDON • SYDNEY • AUCKLAND

BROTHER TO THE LION
A Bantam Spectra Book / May 1988

All rights reserved.
Copyright © 1988 by Rose Estes.
Cover art copyright © 1988 by Pamela Lee.
Map copyright © 1988 by Tom Wham.
No part of this book may be reproduced or transmitted
in any form or by any means, electronic or mechanical,
including photocopying, recording, or by any information
storage and retrieval system, without permission in writing
from the publisher.
For information address: Bantam Books.

ISBN 0-553-27213-6

Published simultaneously in the United States and Canada

PRINTED IN THE UNITED STATES OF AMERICA

KR   0 9 8 7 6 5 4 3 2 1

This book is fondly dedicated to Tommy Thompson of the *Houston Press*, Charlie Evans and Lou Boyd of the *Houston Chronicle*, Jack Long and Downs Matthews of *The Humble Way*, editors and mentors who tried to show me the way.

The research for this book and its two companion novels was greatly aided by help from Diane Gabriel, Assistant Curator of Paleontology and Kurt Hallin, Scientific Assistant at the Milwaukee Public Museum. Also extremely helpful was the medical knowledge, keen comments and extreme patience of Doctor R. V. Both, DVM, Lake Geneva, Wisconsin. Also, I depended greatly on Peggy Hayes's vast knowledge of young wild animals and their relationship to Man.

Lastly, if there are any mistakes, their information is not to blame but rather my interpretation.

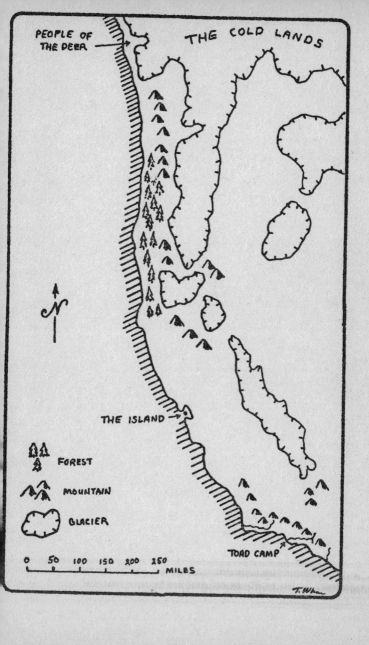

THE COLD LANDS

PEOPLE OF
THE DEER →

THE ISLAND →

TOAD CAMP →

🌲🌲
🌲 FOREST

⛰️⛰️ MOUNTAIN

☁️ GLACIER

0   50   100 150 200 250
|————————————————————————|
                      MILES

T. Wm

CHAPTER ONE

They were being followed. He was sure of it. At first Emri had been uncertain, thinking it but a trick of light and shadows, but now he knew it was so. Shading his eyes against the glare of the sun, he gazed back in the direction from which they had come. There! Dimly outlined against the dark blue shadows where the earth touched the sky, he saw the small figure that he had come to expect.

It seemed that there was only one person, but Emri could not be sure. The follower had remained far behind them, at times lost below the dark line of the horizon.

Though Emri had taken steps to lose the man—wading through streams, climbing rocks that left no trace of their passage, and sweeping the long, soft grass with a leafy branch—nothing had worked. Always, the figure returned, dogging them relentlessly, yet drawing no closer.

Emri and his companions were close to exhaustion, but still he kept them moving, hoping to avoid a confrontation that he knew they could not hope to win.

The three of them were an odd group and their chances for survival were slim even without a fight, for the forces of nature were powerful and would crush a man if he made but a single mistake.

Emri had seen more than twenty summers fade into autumn, and knew that he possessed better-than-average skills with a spear and was a fair shot with a sling. But while he was tall and rangy, he had yet to develop the bulk and brawn that could only come with

1

years of throwing spears, wielding massive clubs, and carrying heavy game.

Emri glanced over at his companion, trying to see him as an enemy might. What he saw was not encouraging.

Hawk had seen only fifteen summers, and, due perhaps to a lack of strength-giving meat, was smaller and more slender than his years warranted. His eyes were bright and alert and his nose was high and thin and beaked, like the bird of prey for which he had been named. His cheekbones were high and slanted, and his face narrowed to a point that always seemed poised to ask a question.

Warmed by the exertion of running, Hawk, like Emri, wore only a small loinskin tied round his slender hips. The rest of his clothing—furs and skins tanned and worked during the Cold Time—were tied in a long bundle, wrapped around his small pile of personal possessions and slung across his back.

Hawk would not give a moment's pause to an enemy, and that would be a mistake. For while the youngster did not appear to be much of a threat, Emri knew that his heart was as fierce as that of the most dangerous predator.

Though Hawk was a fair spearsman and a dead shot with a sling, his true skills lay in his artistic abilities. Time and again Emri had watched Hawk sketch plants and animals so real he had expected them to come to life.

But such talents would not protect them from the spears of an attacker. Nor would the third member of their small party.

Emri looked down at Mosca and grinned. Even though the lion cub was fast approaching the midpoint of his first year, he was still a cub and, as such, often exhibited bursts of childlike behavior.

Even now, exhausted though he was and pushed far beyond his limits, the cub was pouncing up and down on a tuft of grass, batting it from paw to paw as though it were alive.

Emri smiled as he watched the tawny body, now as heavy as a child of ten summers, and remembered the tiny ball of blue-eyed fluff that he and Hawk had found after they fought and killed its mother in a battle for their lives.

He and Hawk still wore the scars of that battle, raised pink lines that scored the dark brown skin of chest and arm and would be a part of them for the rest of their years.

There was as yet no sign of the mane that Mosca would wear as he grew older, but other signs were there. The canines, which would one day be as long as a man's hand, had crept below the bottom of his upper lip; his forelegs had lengthened and begun to develop some of the musculature that would one day enable him to pull down a full-grown stag or a baby tusker.

The hind legs were quite a different matter, for unlike the cub's larger relative, the saber-toothed tiger, the hind legs, that portion below the thigh, were not fixed in an upright position. Rather, they lay flat to the ground, like those of a rabbit, pulling the spine and hind end down, giving adult lions the appearance of walking nearly upright. Even the cub's tail was strange, a short stubby affair that had none of the lithe grace of the tiger's longer tail.

Not exactly a fearsome trio, Emri thought with a sigh as he tried to increase their pace. Their only hope seemed to lie in the possibility of outwitting or eluding their pursuer.

"Emri, we must stop soon," said Hawk, breaking into Emri's worried thoughts. "We've been moving since daybreak and my stomach is growling and my legs are crying for rest."

Emri slowed his pace and then stopped. He could feel his own muscles quivering and shaking as he bent over, resting his hands on his knees, and sucked in great gulps of air. He knew that Hawk was right.

He collapsed wearily on the ground, followed by Hawk, who heaved a grateful sigh. Mosca flopped down between them and rolled over on his back, exposing the soft cream of his underbelly to the warm sun.

Emri dug in the folds of his bundle, which hung suspended from his shoulder by a thong, and extracted three chunks of smoked meat, taken from the carcass of a young tusker some four days earlier. He handed one piece to Hawk and tossed the other to Mosca, who sneezed violently and then fell upon it, crunching through bone and gristle as easily as he would a blade of grass.

Emri chewed his own piece more slowly, even though his stomach was tight with hunger. He savored the taste of the sweet tender meat and knew that it was the very last of their provisions. Now they could add hunger to their flight, for there would be no time to hunt with the tracker on their trail. They would be forced to rely on whatever they could gather as they traveled. It was possible, even likely, that they would be able to bring down small game with a sling, but they would have to eat it raw. They could not afford the time required to start a fire and cook the meat.

"Emri, who do you think is following us?" asked Hawk as he wolfed down the last of the meat and sucked the marrow from the bone.

"I don't know," answered Emri. They had asked each other the same question many times since the man had first appeared, and still there was no answer.

"What are we going to do, Emri?" asked Hawk. "We cannot keep this pace up much longer. Mosca is not used to traveling for such long periods. He is tiring and he has grown much too big for us to carry."

"We must either lose this one somehow or kill him," said Emri. "Do you know this land at all?"

"I have not been at this place before," replied Hawk, looking at the lush, flowing grasslands that surrounded them. "But we are coming to the river. It is just ahead of us. Can you not smell it?"

Emri lifted his head and sucked in the cool moist air, allowing it to pass over his tongue, tasting as well as smelling, and sorting out the information that it carried.

The overwhelming sense was that of vegetation, newly sprung from the earth, freed from the death that was the Cold Time. Next he scented the earth itself, rich and black and fecund. Then there were the animals. The rank, urine scent of the large cats filled his nostrils, as well as the fetid smell of camels. The dung-stink of bison was present, as was the warm, grassy aroma of antelope, overlaid by the heavy, clinging smell of the huge tuskers. And there, faint, yet identifiable, was the heavier taste of water mingled with the stink of mud and rotting fish.

"The Endless Waters lie there," said Hawk, pointing due west. "And the river is directly ahead of us," he added, pointing north. "Perhaps we will be able to rid ourselves of this person by walking along the edge of the water and hiding the marks of our passage."

"That will not be enough," said Emri as he turned back to stare at the unseen follower. "He would find us somehow. We must do more. We must cross the river."

"Cross the river?" Hawk repeated in a puzzled manner. "But that is not possible, Emri. We cannot do this."

"But we must," said Emri, turning back to face Hawk. "That is the only way we will be able to lose this person who clings to our trail. He will not expect us to do such a thing."

"And with good reason," said Hawk. "The river is dangerous at this time, Emri. You saw it when it was low in its banks and slow-running; now it is filled to overflowing with the waters that melt from the mountains at the end of Cold Time.

"The banks are lost beneath the water and they are deep and icy cold, and roar and growl as they rush by. My people leave their homes and move to the high ground. To stay is to die."

Emri was surprised that they had the sense to do that, for Hawk had been born into the Toad clan, a lowly and ignorant tribe, despised by all others, who existed on the edge of starvation and extinction. It was a constant source of wonder to Emri that his clever and talented friend could have emerged from such a tribe.

"It is for this very reason that we must do so," said Emri. "For I fear that is the only way we will escape this man. Nothing else has shaken him from our trail."

"But, Emri, how will we cross?" asked Hawk, obviously fearful at the prospect. "The waters will drag us down and suck the life from us."

"I don't know," Emri answered truthfully. "We will

have to decide when the time comes." Then, without waiting for the argument he knew would follow, Emri picked up his spear and rose, forcing his stiffening limbs into a run.

Mosca bounded along beside him. Then, uttering the peculiar coughing grunt that lions use to communicate among themselves, the cub passed Emri, plunging into the dense, waist-high grass that stretched before them as far as the eye could see.

They continued on for the remainder of the day, stopping only when darkness fell. By that time, the mysterious tracker was lost to sight—although Emri would not allow himself to believe that they had lost him. They were too easy to follow, their passage through the long grass easily distinguishable as a dark line against the softer green.

The land was crowded with new life after the hardships of Cold Time. They killed a long-necked stork as it stalked the shallow waters of a small pond, probing the tall reeds that lined the banks with its long pointed beak in search of the tiny fish and frogs that hid there.

It was Emri's intent to eat the bird raw, since a fire would be easily spotted on this open expanse and would announce their location to the enemy. But Hawk protested, arguing that their presence was no real secret. The tracker could find them by simply following their trail, and so knew their approximate location just as they could guess his.

Realizing that Hawk's arguments were likely correct, and not relishing the fishy taste of the bird's flesh, Emri gave in. He quickly started a fire using his fire-starting sticks, a bit of milkweed fluff hoarded from before the Cold Time, and, once the wood had begun to glow, a careful pinch of powdered wood shavings.

Crouched in the long grass, Emri felt certain that the tiny flame could not be seen from any distance, but he knew that the scent of the roasting meat would hang heavy on the cool night air, pinpointing their location more surely than the largest of fires.

As they huddled round the small fire waiting for the bird to roast, they heard the deep, coughing grunt, *hhunnn, hunnn, hunnnn* of a lion on the hunt and drew closer to the flames. For while they had reared Mosca from his earliest days and had lived through the Cold Time with a pride of cave lions, they knew that they had no claim to immunity from any of the large saber-toothed cats who roamed these plains in search of prey.

Hawk shivered as the cat grunted again, and poked another flat cake of dried bison dung into the fire. The flames leaped up, long blue fingers reaching toward the dark night sky as the fire fed on the dry dung, yellow sparks cracking and sizzling as tiny hidden pockets of moisture were consumed.

"*Aowww, aooww, aowww,*" wailed the cat, its cries diminishing as it slunk away to find easier prey.

"That's it, Hawk!" cried Emri, his eyes large in the flickering light. "We'll start a fire! The grass is too wet to burn well, but there will be lots of smoke and it will give us time to get away. Our tracks will be lost, and if we're lucky, he'll never find us!"

"But what if we're not lucky?" asked Hawk, his high, slanted cheekbones and dark glittering eyes highlighted by the fire, making him appear older, harder.

"It will work," cried Emri. "The winds blow off of the Endless Waters as well as toward us as they are doing now. The fire will travel away from us and toward the tracker, of this I am sure."

"I do not like the thought of being caught by the flames," said Hawk, looking away from Emri. "I would not like to die roasting in the fire like a piece of meat."

"Would you rather die on the spear of the one who follows?" asked Emri. "That is no friend out there. If he catches us, he will not ask to our health. He will kill us. I know it and so do you.

"We have only three choices, Hawk. We can stand and fight, and probably die. We can try to lose him . . . or we can kill him first. I will do nothing unless you agree, so say what it is to be."

"We are no rabbits to run before this man," Hawk said fiercely, turning back to face Emri. "Do you forget that we are brothers to the lion and have killed a great saber-tooth tiger! Why do we run? I say, let us stand and fight!"

"Well spoken, my brother," said Emri, leaning forward and placing his hand on Hawk's shoulder. "But we are only two, and neither of us is well versed in the ways of fighting.

"When we fought the great tiger, we were not alone and our brothers, the lions, had drawn much of the tiger's blood. He was badly weakened from the sickness that had poisoned his mind and body, and even then he killed four of our brothers and nearly took your life as well.

"It is not lack of courage that fashions my words, Hawk. I do not wish to fight this man, for I do not want to risk any of our lives. I have lost my clan, my family, and she whom I love, as well as our brothers, the lions. I would be truly alone if anything happened to you or Mosca."

Emri stared into Hawk's eyes and saw the fight drain out of them. The boy lowered his head and stroked the cub's soft fur as he lay sleeping close to the edge of the fire.

"We are family, Hawk. We have no one except each other now, and if one of us is hurt or killed, it could easily mean the death of all. And what of Mosca? He is as yet too young to fend for himself; without us he would die."

"Forgive me. Anger made my words, not thought," said Hawk. "We will do as you say, Emri. How will we set this fire?—for as you have said, the land is still wet from the Cold Time."

"There is much green stuff, that is true," said Emri as he dug his fingers into the thick, matted vegetation at the base of the long grass and wrenched it free. "But look here: under the new growth is dried stuff that died during the Cold Time. I think that it will burn, and when it is hot enough, it will eat even the new growth and there will be much smoke."

Emri tossed the handful of debris into the fire where it burned brightly for an instant and then was gone. Hawk turned admiring eyes on Emri, the fire reflected in his pupils as he nodded his agreement.

"Let us do this thing now, Emri," he said softly. "The one who follows may be sneaking up on us even as we speak, or he may be resting as we are. If we fire the grass now, we will have the darkness of the night to aid our plan. The light of day might show him some manner of escape. If we would do this, then let us do it well."

Emri did not speak for a moment, mulling the thought over in his mind. Finally, he raised his head and nodded.

"This is a good plan. We will do it." He held his hand up above the level of the grass and then lowered it.

"The wind is steady, blowing toward us as it often does at night. This will suit us well. Come, my friend, let us begin. Take care that we are not separated, for fire calls no man his brother and would feed on our bones as happily as it would those of our enemy."

Fixing their bundles firmly on their backs and waking the sleeping cub, Emri and Hawk each took up a fiery brand and set off into the night.

CHAPTER TWO

The night was ablaze.
Flames shot high into the air leaping from one small
bush to the next, feeding on the dry, matted debris that
lay thick on the ground, the product of many seasons of
growth and death.

There was much smoke, rising so thick and heavy as
to nearly obscure the flames. And then there was the
heat, almost stifling, ready to suck the air out of one's
lungs if one ventured too close.

All around them there was noise; the roaring of the
fire, the popping and sizzling and anguished wail of
moisture boiling within the stems and leaves of living
plants, and the frantic cries of the animals trapped
behind the conflagration.

The thunder of hooves was everywhere. Terrified
antelope raced out of the flames; tall stags with towering
racks of antlers bounded past with singed pelts; small
cats with wild eyes; and once a huge lumbering black
bear shepherding a tinier version of itself shambled past.

The fire had been difficult to start, but they had
been persistent, touching their torches to anything that
would burn—dried dung, dead branches, and withered
weeds killed by the Cold Time. At last it had taken hold
and started to spread by itself. Emri and Hawk had
stopped and watched the natural evolution of what they
had begun. But the results were far more frightening
than they had imagined as the flames rushed across the
soft rolling grasslands, consuming everything that stood
in its path.

Hardest to bear were the terrified shrieks and

tormented cries of the animals trapped in the blaze. Emri had not stopped to think of the many small creatures that had been born since the end of Cold Time. They were being caught and killed by the flames, much as he had hoped to kill the one who followed them.

The sky was red and gold and white with the reflection of the fire, and Emri stared at his handiwork as the air rang with the thunder of hooves milling in all directions and the screams of animals maddened by fear and pain.

Hawk turned to Emri, his eyes wide with sorrow. "I—I did not realize . . ." he stammered. "I did not stop to think about the animals. I did not know there were so many."

"Nor did I," answered Emri. "Many will die to-night. All we can hope is that our enemy is among them. Come, let us go. There is nothing more that we can do, and I fear the fire. See there: that tongue of flame pokes forward, goes against the wind. I would not like to be burned by this fire of our own making."

Mosca was huddled at the far edge of the circle of light, moaning and shivering with fear; he was all too happy to move away from the fire as Emri and Hawk began the slow, easy lope that would take them many miles before morning.

Even now as the distance grew, they could hear the fire and the cries of the animals held behind its lines. They were forced to keep an alert eye as large wild-eyed herds of bison and deer galloped past. Once, a badly burned hare hopped in front of them and then stood still, rubbing scorched, blinded eyes with paws that were bare of fur. Emri clubbed the pathetic creature, freeing its spirit, enabling it to travel on to the next world.

They traveled through the night, ignoring the ache of exhaustion that filled their muscles and the dullness that clouded their minds. . . .

Thick gray smoke swirled up around them with every step, and Emri wondered dully if the wind had shifted and was carrying the fire toward them. He turned and looked around him and noted that the whiteness

cloaking the ground was merging with the sky around
them. Only then did his exhausted mind understand that
dawn had come, shrouding the land as it did each
morning with heavy mists. Twice he stumbled and
nearly went down, unable to see the ground beneath his
feet. Realizing that it would be folly to continue, he held
up his hand, signifying a halt.

Hawk sank to the ground immediately, wrapping his
arms around Mosca, who was too tired to even moan his
displeasure.

"Not here in the open, Hawk. Over there by that
tree; it'll give us more shelter," urged Emri, pointing
toward a massive oak that loomed up out of the mist, its
huge twisted branches outlined against the white sky.

They had to carry Mosca, who refused to rise from
where he lay on the ground panting. Between them,
they carried the tawny cat to the base of the tree and
there they were grateful to find a deep depression
between the great gnarled roots, filled with leaves and
litter from the previous season. They dug a hole deep
enough to accommodate the three of them, barely
managing to scrape a layer of leaves over themselves
before they fell back and gave themselves over to sleep.

Emri wakened slowly to a soft warmth on his face.
For a moment, he pictured the soft brown eyes and
warm body of Dawn, she who was to have been his
woman had he remained with his tribe. But then the
picture faded abruptly as the gentle warmth turned to
wet snuffling, complete with the prick and scrape of stiff
bristles moving across his cheek.

Emri opened his eyes and gazed into the limpid
brown eyes of a water pig, its long flexible snout moving
across his face with the delicacy of a spider's touch. For a
moment they stared at each other, then Emri sat up with
a brittle scattering of dead leaves and the water pig
squealed and trotted away, a tiny brown-and-white
spotted replica cantering at her heels.

Emri grinned as he stood up, brushing the scratchy
bits of clinging leaves from his body. Water pigs—that
meant water. Maybe they were near the river.

Mosca and Hawk still slept, curled around each other, exhausted from the long night's work. Emri covered them more completely with leaves, hiding them from all but the closest of scrutiny, and then set out, following the deep pointed indentations of the water pig's hooves, hoping that they would lead him to water.

The mist had lifted, burned off by the heat of the rising sun which now stood directly overhead.

Although Emri could still smell the smoke from the night's fire, the air was clear and crisp and the land was untouched. The fire had traveled in the opposite direction, as he had hoped.

There were trees everywhere, some huge and gnarled like the one they had 'sheltered under, which Emri now recognized as an oak of the type that dropped acorns in the Gathering Time. There were also a number of trees with shaggy red bark that rose tall and straight to the sky, as well as a wide variety of smaller trees. The ground underfoot was damp and springy with thick clumps of bright green moss. Stands of tall plumed grass, some taller than Emri himself, arched overhead.

There was the sound of movement and Emri dropped into a crouch, reversing his grip on his spear so that he would be ready to throw should the maker of the sound materialize.

The noise came again; it was the crack of breaking branches. Moving silently, Emri crept forward and parted the foliage of a dense bush. Some twenty paces away was a huge shaggy ground sloth gnawing on the ends of a willow branch. Chewing the last of the tender leaves, the immense creature stood up on its hind legs and reached for another branch, hooking it with huge curved claws, each one longer than Emri's own hand and as sharp as the edge of a newly knapped blade.

There was a soft tremulous bleat and Emri saw a tiny copy of the gigantic creature wobbling beneath her shaggy belly. Its eyes were still wide and dewy, with the look of one newly born. Its soft nose butted at its mother's side and fumbled through the coarse fur until it fastened on a teat.

The mother had succeeded in grasping another

branch. She pulled it down until she was able to lean on it with her chest, using the weight of her body to break the branch from the trunk. It parted with a sharp snap, blending in with the outraged squeal of the infant who had been dislodged from its hold.

The female located the tender tips of the branch by scent rather than by sight—for her small rheumy eyes were not capable of seeing clearly—and she began to feed contentedly, wrapping her peculiar prehensile snout and lips around the soft shoots.

Emri listened to the soft, contented humming sound that came from the young one as its belly filled with rich creamy milk.

Emri allowed the branches to fall, and moved away quietly so as not to alarm the great creature whose hearing was far more acute than its eyesight.

He knew that he would have been able to kill the ground sloth, for, despite her sharp claws, she was often unable to protect herself against the cats and dire wolves who considered her tasty fare, being totally deficient in the rage and anger that should have caused her to fight back, protecting her young as well as her life.

Emri had often watched as the men of his tribe slaughtered the gentle giants and wondered why the Gods had made such a creature without the ability to protect its own life. He himself felt there was something shameful in killing such an animal, and left it to seek other game.

A fat hare browsing among a patch of pale shoots provided more acceptable fare, and after a short, frenetic chase, Emri brought the animal down with a well-placed stone from his sling. He returned to the spot where he had first found the hare and broke off several handfuls of the pale stalks that the hare had been nibbling. Emri had learned the value of such groundfoods from Hawk, who had taught him that the plants were capable of keeping a man alive when no game was to be found. Emri did not recognize the stalks, but perhaps Hawk would.

Carrying the hare by its long floppy ears, Emri

returned to the tree where Hawk and Mosca still slept under their covering of leaves.

Feeling content, and all but certain that they had lost the one who had followed them, Emri gathered a small pile of dead dry wood and set about making a fire.

Mosca wakened with a great yawn that terminated in a high-pitched squeak reminiscent of the days of his cubhood. Emri tousled the young cat's head and was butted in the chest as Mosca expressed his affection. Emri was forced to put out a hand to steady himself, so great was the cat's strength, a reminder of his rapid growth.

Emri propped the skinned and gutted hare on a green stick above the fire and turned to study the strange groundfoods he had picked.

They were odd, unlike anything he had seen before, pure white, the color of grubs, the thickness of his forefinger and as long as his hand. They were completely without leaves, smooth for their entire length until the end where they coiled snugly like the curve of a snail shell.

Emri sniffed them curiously and was rewarded by the earthy smell of fungus. He nibbled gingerly on a stalk with his teeth and tasted nothing but a slight green bitterness that was rather unpleasant. Thinking he had made a mistake, he drew back his arm to cast them away.

"Don't do that, you'll just have to pick them up again," said a sleepy voice.

Emri turned to see Hawk watching him lazily from his bed of leaves.

"Those are curly tails," said Hawk, slowly unwinding with much stretching of his stiffened limbs. He stood up amid a shower of crushed leaves and tottered out to take the white stalks from Emri's hand.

"Here, wrap them in some wet leaves and bury them in the embers, and soon after, you'll be licking your fingers and wishing for more," said Hawk. "I'll go find the leaves—I need to see if my legs still work. I think they died sometime during the night. I feel like an old one, Emri. Tell me that we lost our follower. I would hate to think that I feel this bad for no good reason."

"I have not sought high ground to find out," said
Emri with a smile. "But I cannot imagine that he
escaped the flames. You saw how fast they traveled. If he
was not killed, at the very least he was forced to run
before them, in a direction opposite from that which we
have taken."

"Emri, you and I have lived, long beyond the time
that anyone would have guessed, through strange and
most unusual circumstances," said Hawk. "Do you think
it wise to believe that we are the only people who might
be so favored by the Gods?"

"You are right," said Emri, much chastened by his
younger companion's wisdom and disturbed that he had
not thought of it himself. By such mistakes did a man
die. As Hawk turned away to find the leaves with which
to wrap the pale stalks, Emri picked up his spear and set
off to find high ground from which he might observe the
land behind them.

This task proved more difficult than he had thought,
for the land was dense with foliage, much of which grew
taller than Emri's head, and it was impossible to gain any
clear view of the land. Finally, Emri found a tall red-
barked tree and, leaving his spear propped against the
base, quickly scaled the trunk.

The rough bark made for easy climbing and Emri
ascended quickly until he found a perch on a large
branch more than halfway up the tree.

From his vantage point it was easy to see the
charred lands stretching to the horizon, which was all
but obscured by a dark, smoky pall. Emri shivered,
stunned by how far the fire had traveled and by the
extent of damage it had caused. It seemed all but
impossible that anyone had lived through such a fire.

Emri scanned the dark smoking land for a long time
and thought he saw some little movement; closer study
proved it to be animals—apparently critically injured, by
their jerky movements. There was nothing to be seen of
the mysterious human.

Emri was relieved, yet worried. He wondered if
perhaps they should say the words that would speed the
man's spirit to the land of their ancestors.

Enemy or not, it was hard to think of a spirit wandering the world without a home. And such a thing could be dangerous as well, for the spirit of a dead one could seek out the person responsible for its death, enter the body through ear or mouth or nostril, and still their heart out of revenge.

Emri slid down the tree, retrieved his spear, and hurried back to camp to share his thoughts with Hawk.

Hawk had just finished turning the hare as Emri burst through the bushes. Mosca was leaning forward, paw extended as though to remove the meat from the spit, and Hawk left off chastising him as he saw the worried look on his friend's face.

"What troubles you?" Hawk asked quickly, leaping to his feet and reaching for his spear. "Does he follow still?"

"No, no. There is no sight of a follower," said Emri. "But that is the problem. If he is dead, his spirit might well be searching for us. We must say the words that will send the spirit out of this world and into the land of our ancestors before it seeks to kill us."

"I did not think," whispered Hawk, clearly shaken by the terrible thought as he peered up into the air, squinting his eyes as though it might help him see the spirit more clearly.

"Here, let us say the words," said Emri as he lifted a small chunk of burning wood out of the fire and set it apart.

Hawk glanced about the small clearing until he spotted a bit of sweet grass, which would represent green, growing life, and quickly picked a handful.

Emri sliced off a bit of the hare with his knife and then laid it carefully alongside the small flame where it would burn yet not extinguish the fire.

"Spirit, take this meat that you may eat in the land of our ancestors and never be hungry," chanted Emri.

"Spirit, take these greens that you may never want for groundfoods," whispered Hawk.

"Spirit, take this offering of our blood that you may still your wish for vengence and live happily among the ancestors. We bid you go in peace," said Emri. He sliced his finger with the knife and allowed the blood to flow onto the fire, where it sizzled and steamed. Emri handed the knife to Hawk, who took it with a startled expression yet followed Emri's lead repeating both action and words exactly.

"There," said Emri with a deep sigh as he turned away from the fire. "I hope that it was enough. I've never killed a man before."

Hawk held his finger and looked down into the fire, his face long with sorrow. "And I hope that we never have to do it again. It makes my heart heavy. Let us leave this place, Emri. I do not wish to be here."

Looking around the small clearing that had seemed so pleasant such a short time before, Emri felt a chill pass down his spine and realized that he too was anxious to leave the place behind.

It took but a moment to pluck the half-cooked hare from the fire, unearth the groundfoods, and stamp out the fire. Then they were gone, traveling north toward the river and wondering what they would find.

CHAPTER THREE

Hawk had not exaggerated. The river was twice as wide as the last time Emri had seen it, and was far from being the sluggish, slow-moving body of water he remembered. It thundered past at a dizzying rate, a peculiar shade of milky brown clotted with swirling patches of dirty white foam.

Small trees and broken branches tumbled over and over in the turbulent water, forcefully reminding Emri of another experience with a small friendly stream that had become a raging torrent. He and Hawk and Mosca had come close to losing their lives during that encounter and he was unwilling to try such a thing again.

Mosca must have had similar memories for he began to moan, *aowaugh, aowaugh*; a sound that came from deep in his chest and expressed his deepest displeasure. He swayed from side to side, his head held low, and then backed up, removing himself further and further from the water.

Emri felt his confidence fall as he gazed at the great expanse of water. Hawk was right. There seemed to be no way to cross the river. He could see the other side plainly, yet he could not even imagine a way for them to reach its banks.

His thoughts were interrupted as part of the bank crumbled in front of them, fell into the river, and was instantly swallowed by the rampaging water.

Emri and Hawk backed up quickly, retreating from the hungry waters that chewed at the banks continuously, as though angry at the limits they placed.

"Never have I seen the river so high," Hawk said

wonderingly. "The Water Gods must be angry with the land to punish it so."

"Let us hope their anger does not extend to people," said Emri, not at all certain that such would be the case. The water showed no preference for man or land and was always willing to swallow either. "We shall make an offering and beg for safe passage."

"I do not understand why we must cross the river," said Hawk as they settled themselves at the base of a tree a safe distance from the water.

"Where else is there for us to go?" asked Emri with a shrug. "Your people will not take us in even if we wanted to go to them. Since they believe you were killed, they insist you are a vengeful spirit."

"I would not go to them in any case," Hawk said, and spat upon the ground. "They are stupid and think only of themselves and their bellies."

Emri held his tongue, knowing that it was true. Believing Hawk dead, the Toads had excluded Hawk's mother from a share of the tribal pot. She had died, a victim no doubt from the pain of being shunned as well as from the starvation that had finally claimed her.

Hawk's return had done nothing to convince the tribe that they had made a mistake. Not wanting to be proved wrong, they had chosen to believe that Hawk was a spirit rather than a live person. They had greeted Emri, Hawk, and Mosca's appearance with a barrage of stones and sticks, and chased them from the dismal camp.

"Nor can we go to your tribe," said Hawk. "Mandris, the shaman, will have turned your tribe against us by now, telling them that we killed the great tiger who is the totem of your tribe."

"Of course Mandris will not mention *his* part in the story," Emri said bitterly. "He will not tell them that the tiger was sick and dying and in terrible pain. Nor will he admit that he controlled the tiger's actions through the use of pain-killing herbs.

"He will not admit that he killed my father so that he might take his place as chief of the tribe. Nor was he content with taking my mother to wife, but sought to kill me as well to ensure his place of power," Emri said.

"He will not tell the people that he directed the tiger to kill us and that we only fought to protect our own lives," added Hawk.

"No," Emri said heavily. "We will be cursed at the campfires of the Tigers. There is no place for us there."

"I do not understand why we did not stay with the lions, Emri. We were happy there."

"We could not have stayed there either, Hawk, my friend, and you know it in your head if not in your heart.

"After the tiger killed Leader and Beauty and One Eye, Long Tooth became chief of the pride. He had no love for us, and had we stayed, he would have killed us."

"I miss them," mumbled Hawk as he rubbed Mosca's ears. "The cubs especially. They were like family."

"We must find another family to belong to," Emri said gently, knowing that Hawk was still feeling the pain of the death of the lions who had been their friends. The ache was still strong in his own heart.

"We must find a tribe to make our own before Cold Time comes again," said Emri. "Two alone stand little chance of survival. We must find others who will accept us and value us for what we can offer.

"I believe that we must take ourselves far from this place. Mandris will waste no time in telling of the death of the totem and soon all tribes within reach of his tongue will know his version of the story. Even if they do not actively seek to kill us, they will certainly shun us and, worse, inform the shaman of our presence."

"But the land across the river is unknown," said Hawk, lifting his eyes to search the distant horizon. "I know of no one who has ever been there."

"So much the better," said Emri. "It will be a place for a new beginning where no one will have heard our story or Mandris's lies."

"We must wait until the river slows before we cross," said Hawk, "and that will not be until the long days of Warm Time."

"We cannot wait that long," said Emri. "Toads are not entirely stupid. Our presence will be noted, and somehow, word will reach Mandris and we will be forced to flee again. I say we go now at a time and place of our own choosing, rather than run before the spears of the Tigers."

"But how, Emri? How do we cross the river?" persisted Hawk. "There is no way!"

"There must be a way," Emri said grimly. "It is up to us to find it. Tell me about the place where the river meets the Endless Waters. What is that like?"

"It is a dangerous place, far more dangerous than the river itself," said Hawk. "The water has much strength there. Perhaps that is where the Water God makes his home, for the water is never quiet. The River God pushes down and forces his brown water far out into the blue of the Endless Waters. Then the God of the Endless Waters shoves back and sends the waves far up the river until they lose their strength. And then it begins again."

"Is it always like that? Are the waters never still?" asked Emri.

"Sometimes the waters grow tired of fighting, and lie heavy and nearly still, neither pushing nor shoving in either direction," Hawk admitted.

"Could a man not make his way across the river at that time?" asked Emri.

"Oh no, never!" said Hawk, a look of fear crossing his face. "High or low, push or shove, the mouth of the river is always filled with biters!"

"Biters?" said Emri, the term meaning nothing to him.

"Yes! Biters! Have you never heard of them?" asked Hawk, appearing astounded at his friend's ignorance. "Here, this is what they look like." Seizing a bit of stick, he smoothed a patch of soft damp earth and quickly drew the shape of a large fish with a high fin projecting from the top of its back and a gaping mouth filled with jagged teeth.

"This is a biter, Emri. They can eat a child in a

single gulp and cut a man in half. Many of our people are taken by biters as they tend their nets even though we watch for them most carefully. They are the tigers of the water."

"And these biters are to be found at the mouth of the river," Emri said.

"Always," said Hawk. "I think they wait there taking their pick of the fish who are swept up and down the river and hoping for a man stupid enough to cross."

"All right, my friend," Emri said with a sigh. "You and your biters have convinced me. We'll have to find another way across."

Studying his friend's disconsolate expression, Hawk said hesitantly, "Of course, there're always the floaters."

"What floaters?" Emri asked wearily as he sat slumped against the tree, one arm covering his eyes, shielding them from the sun.

"The floaters that my people use to cross the river while tending their nets and fishing lines," said Hawk, already beginning to regret his words.

Emri sat bolt upright and stared at Hawk. "Your people know how to cross the river? Why did you not tell me this before?"

"Because I do not wish to go," said Hawk, hanging his head and jabbing at the earth with the point of his stick. "I have heard that there are terrible Gods on the other side of the river who fight each other with mountains of ice, and that any man who dares to venture there will be turned to ice and never return."

"Are you afraid, my brother?" asked Emri in amazement. "I have never known you to be afraid."

"A man is wise to fear the Gods, Emri," replied Hawk. "I am not afraid of things that I can see and feel and touch, things that I know about. Yes, I am afraid and I do not want to go to this unknown land."

"Yet you have told me of a way to cross the river," Emri said wonderingly.

"I see that you are determined to go with or without my help," said Hawk. "We are brothers, we three, brothers to the lion. You are my family. If you are determined to cross the river, then I must go with you."

"Tell me about the floaters," said Emri, his eyes shining with emotion as well as excitement.

Wiping away the outline of the biter, Hawk began to draw once more.

"First the men find long straight trees, twice as tall as a man yet, no thicker than his wrist. They bend the tree back and forth until it breaks off at the base. Then they strip away all of the side branches until they have one long pole.

"When they have three such poles of the same length, they lash them together tightly with wet leather and bend and fashion the poles until they take on the shape they want, like so."

Emri watched closely as Hawk sketched three lines that looked like the bottom half of a nutshell, pointed at both ends and slightly rounded on the sides and bottom.

"Once the poles have dried in this shape and the leather has drawn tight, they cover the frame with the skin of a water beast. This skin is very tough, yet floats upon the water like the wind. It must be the skin that keeps the animal afloat while alive."

"What is this water beast you speak of?" asked Emri. "Is it another like the biter?"

"No." Hawk laughed. "Water beasts are the most favorite food of biters. They have teeth but they are of no use against biters or even man. Surely you have seen them. They live along the shores of the Endless Waters in great numbers and spend their days swimming and leaping through the water, catching fish, and sunning themselves on the rocks. I have moved among them. They have no fear of man, and it is easy to come close and even touch the small ones when their mothers are not near. That is how our men kill them for their skins."

"If they are easy to approach, we can eat them," said Emri, his thoughts never far from the ever-present need for food.

"I do not wish to eat them if we can find other food," said Hawk. "They are too trusting; it feels like killing a person. I do not like the look in their eyes. The men of my tribe thought me a fool for saying such things. They had no problem killing the water beasts, but I cannot do so."

Emri said nothing, remembering his own feelings for the ground sloth. It seemed that he and Hawk were both misfits, for no man of the Tigers shrank from killing easy prey. Softness was a weakness that could lead to death. It was an emotional luxury that could not be afforded.

"The land is rich with food now," said Emri. "I see no reason for us to kill a water beast while there are so many other animals to choose from. Now finish telling me about this strange thing, this floater. What happens next?"

"Well, the men stretch the skin tight across the bottom pole and pull it up over the sides. They make it stick there with a soup made from boiling fish bones. It smells terrible, but it sticks things together and they do not come apart.

"After this is done they wait for the skins to dry, and then cover part of the top, leaving room for the men to sit inside. Depending on the size of the poles, it takes nine or ten skins to cover it completely."

"Then what?" asked Emri, looking at the drawing and trying to visualize how the thing would appear in real life.

"Then the men put it in the water and get inside the skins, which now float on top of the water. They make it go where they want with flat sticks which they push against the water."

"How long would it take us to make such a thing," asked Emri, staring at the strange image as he struggled to comprehend the concept of it.

"We will not make one," said Hawk. "We will take one from the Toads. They owe me much that they can never return. It is my due."

"But, Hawk, have you forgotten what happened the last time we tried to talk to them? They nearly killed us!"

"Yes, but that time, they merely thought that we were spirits; this time we'll make them sure of it. By the time we're done with them, they'll be willing to give us all the floaters in the village and anything else we want, just to get rid of us!"

Emri looked at Hawk's broad smile and grinned in return. "I like it," he said with a laugh. "I like it very much. I always wondered what it was like to be a spirit. Now I guess I'll find out!"

CHAPTER FOUR

They found a patch of slick white clay on the side of a bank and slathered it heavily over their bodies till every bit of skin was covered. Then they rubbed the clay into their hair and ran their fingers through it till it stood up in spikelike tufts all over their heads.

A broad grin creased Emri's face as he studied Hawk. Had he not known that it was his friend, he would easily have believed that he was seeing a spirit.

Hawk pointed at Emri and laughed aloud. "Oh, my brother," he gasped, "you make a very fine spirit walker. I myself am terrified!"

"Too bad it doesn't work on Mosca," muttered Emri, and the cub paced around them growling and whining nervously, shaking his head from side to side.

"Shouldn't Mosca be a spirit as well?" asked Hawk, as he dove for the cub and grabbed him by his front legs.

"It would look strange if he were not," agreed Emri. Digging a handful of clay out of the bank, he began to rub it into the cub's fur. Mosca struggled to get away and nearly succeeded in doing so twice, but finally they were done and the cub looked out at them through clay-caked eyelids and blinked. "*Waughh,*" he bawled piteously, attempting to paw at his nose.

"Ho! Don't let him rub himself until the clay dries, or it will come off," cautioned Hawk. After renewing their own covering, they sat as still as possible, preventing the cub from grooming himself until the clay had hardened into a dry coating that clung like a natural growth to skin, hair, and fur.

27

Left to his own devices, Mosca would have rolled on the ground and freed himself of the strange mantle, but Hawk and Emri hurried him up onto the grassy bank that rose above the flowing waters.

Mosca was angry. He swiped out with his paw, batting at Emri with claws unsheathed. He hissed at Hawk, his ears laid back flat against his head.

"Ho, brother! Save your anger and use it against the Toads who are more deserving!" cried Emri as he opened his stride and pulled away from the angry cat.

By late afternoon, they had drawn near to the Toad encampment.

Mosca had quieted, and now contented himself with sullen looks from slitted eyes. Once, in spite of their efforts, the cat had laid upon the ground and rolled in a patch of loose sand. But far from dislodging the clay, some of the sand had adhered to the surface and only served to give the cat an even more peculiar appearance.

Following Mosca's lead, Emri and Hawk rolled themselves in the sand as well, and rose covered with splotches of darker-colored soil that made it look as though their flesh were rotting away. Tiny twigs and bits of grass clung to them and Emri knew that if he looked half as fearsome as Hawk, they would give the Toads a fright they would never forget.

"We must leave our possessions here, Emri. We cannot carry them with us. Spirits do not have possessions," said Hawk, as he laid a hand on Emri's arm.

"We cannot leave our things behind, Hawk," said Emri. "They hold everything we own in this world. If we are not able to return for them, we will need to replace everything: spears, points, fire starters, healing herbs, clothes. It would mean starting over."

"I had not thought of that," said Hawk, his face crinkled with thought as he remembered the long days of painstaking effort that had gone into the making of the precious spearpoints and the suffering that they had endured while they attempted to fashion clothing that would protect them from the terrible cold. It would be hard to leave those things behind.

"Let us roll the bundles in the dust," said Emri.

"Hopefully they will think them spirit bundles. If not, perhaps they will be too terrified to notice at all."

Hawk had his doubts but he kept them to himself.

They found a patch of light-colored soil near the peak of the high rise of land.

As Hank rolled the bundles in the fine dust, sifting it over every wrinkle so as to cover the bundles completely, Emri crept to the edge of the rocks and peered over, taking care that his body was not silhouetted against the sky.

It was as Hawk had said. The Toads had taken shelter from the rising water on a broad ledge on the flank of the hill. Their few possessions were strewn across the rock face without any apparent organization or order. Wood, spears, crude things with fire-hardened tips, had been carelessly left on the ground or stacked against the ragged rock face.

Emri studied the camp carefully, counting the numbers of the opposition.

Of full grown men—and some of these were old and crippled—there appeared to be no more than the number of fingers on both hands. Younger males numbered slightly fewer, and women and children numbered all the fingers on four hands. It was a large number to be faced by so few and Emri began to wonder if their ploy would be successful. Perhaps he had underestimated the Toads.

He watched them, studying them carefully, taking in the smallest details, searching for their weaknesses.

The Toads were not an imposing people. Smaller in size than Tigers, their bodies seemed less strong as well. Their shoulders were slumped and rounded, conveying a feeling of defeat. Their black hair was worn level with the chin, chopped short with the edge of a sharpened shell. It gave their flat, chunky faces a heavy, square look quite unlike Hawk's high-bridged nose and sharp features. Comparing the long, slim graceful limbs of his friend with the short, thick graceless limbs of the Toads, Emri wondered once again if Hawk were not really of some other tribe.

The Toads had chosen a poor place for their camp

from a standpoint of defense, for there was no place for them to go. The river curved along the base of the broad rocky ledge, running fast and perilous with a soft sibilant roar. A narrow trail curled down from the ledge to the edge of the water.

Emri's heart beat faster as he saw the skin floaters. They were just as Hawk had described them. There were three of them lying at the edge of the ledge completely untended.

The ledge could only be reached by way of a steep trail that had been carved out of the face of the hill. Studying the trail, Emri saw that the soil beneath him was but a narrow layer, no more than a handspan thick, covering the skeleton of rock that lay beneath.

The rock face descended in a near-vertical cut from the top of the cliff, which was heaped and mounded with large boulders. Emri saw that at one time the hill had broken in half and had fallen into the river, leaving the exposed rock face and the ledge behind.

The Toads had taken advantage of the disaster and had carved holes in the face of the rock, picking out the broken slabs and using the holes for shelter, like so many rabbits. The pock-marked surface reminded Emri of a rabbit warren and he hoped that the Toads would frighten as easily.

The Toads were involved in a number of activities. Some of the men and boys were fishing, standing at the lowest spit of land where it edged into the water and holding sharpened sticks in readiness.

As Emri watched, one of the men gave a loud cry and plunged his spear into the water with great force. When he pulled it back, a large silvery-scaled fish, more than half the man's length and as broad as a small child, flapped wildly on the end of the stick.

The man hurled the stick up onto the bank, and before the fish could slither back into the river, the women and children were upon it, beating it with sticks and clubs and shouting loudly.

The remaining Toads ceased their various activities and converged on the circle surrounding the fish.

Their shrill cries rose above them like the keening of an eagle on the wing. The man who had speared the fish emerged from the mob clutching the head of the fish and a large portion of the body. A number of children and women followed after him, alternately imploring and showering him with abuse. But he refused to share and clutching the fish to his chest, sat down on a boulder and began to consume it raw, wrenching the flesh free with huge bites and watching the others closely in case they attempted to take it from him. The sounds of his eating as well as the growls that emanated from his throat were clearly heard from Emri's vantage point.

One small child with a wasted frame and bloated belly remained after the others had given up and fought their way back into the throng surrounding the carcass. He hunkered on his thin haunches and crawled closer, ignoring the man's growls. He was within touching distance when the man's foot shot out and caught the child solidly in the ribs.

Emri heard the boy cry out, and then watched in amazement as the child seized the man's leg and sliced it with something held concealed in his hand.

The man screamed and fell backward, his hands reaching instinctively for his leg, attempting to stem the flow of blood that poured from the deep gash.

No sooner had he reached for his leg than the boy reached up, snatched the fish, and hurried away to climb to a position on the rocks that would not bear the weight of a grown man.

The man took several steps, screaming and shaking his fist at the boy. The child ignored him completely, all of his attention being focused on devouring the fish as quickly as possible.

Only a few people bothered to look up from their efforts to obtain a bit of the fish before it was gone, and these merely laughed and pointed their fingers at the man, openly jeering at him for being tricked by a child. The man's face twisted with rage. Emri thought that the boy had best guard his back until the man's anger faded.

Emri closed his ears to the man's cries and instead looked over the area, trying to formulate a plan. The geography was difficult, not lending itself to attack any more than escape. Anyone who climbed down the trail to the camp would be spotted instantly, a helpless target that not even the crude spears of the Toads could miss.

And even if they succeeded in frightening the Toads and entering the camp unharmed, what chance would they have of stealing the floaters and removing them from the ledge? It would be all but impossible to haul them back up the steep rock face. And if they attempted to do so, even the Toads would begin to wonder why the spirits had need of a floating skin. It would be but a short jump of logic to tell them that spirits did not need such things, only men.

The last remaining possibility was that of launching the floaters from the tiny spit of rock that protruded out into the foaming water. Emri shivered as he watched the water race by, and immediately closed his mind to the thought; a man would be dashed to pieces if he were foolish enough to try such a thing. There had to be another way.

"Ah, they are here, just where I thought they would be," said Hawk as he slid into position next to Emri and peered over the rocks at the members of his former tribe.

"They've killed a fish and have been fighting over shares," said Emri.

"As always," Hawk replied with a derisive snort.

"Why do they not cook the fish?" asked Emri. "Animals eat flesh raw, but men do not when they have fire."

"Toads use fire to warm themselves and to keep the insects away," said Hawk, "but food is food and it does not matter to them whether it tastes of the flames or of blood. The flames take longer and give others a chance to steal your share. Raw food is quicker and more likely to end up in your belly rather than someone else's."

"Then how did you learn to cook food, and so well," asked Emri, momentarily distracted from watching the Toads.

"I have always been different," Hawk replied simply. "In this matter as in all others. Food is like drawing to me—thoughts turn themselves around and around in my mind and I must try them. Sometimes it tastes good and sometimes not." Satisfied with this explanation, Emri turned his attention back to the tableau of greed and suspicion below, noting the tiny children foraging among the rocks and dirt for scraps that might have been overlooked by their elders. Such behavior would have been inconceivable among the Tigers.

"See, there are the floaters," said Hawk, pointing to the three objects on the ledge.

"I see them," said Emri. "But how are we to get them away?"

"Uhhh, uhhh," grunted Mosca, and recognizing it as a cry denoting the approach of something of interest, Emri turned and looked over his shoulder. His blood ran cold. There, on the next ridge but a short distance away, was their follower, a dark shape clearly defined against the clear blue sky.

"Hawk!" Emri whispered hoarsely. As Hawk turned, Emri jerked his head toward the man.

"How did he find us? How did he escape the fire!" Hawk cried. "Surely we killed him!" Then a new and even more terrible thought struck him. "Emri, what if it is a real spirit come to kill us?"

"You are acting like a Toad!" Emri said harshly. "Look, you. That is no spirit. It is a man! See how sharply he is outlined against the sky. Look! He sees us! He is waving his hand and now he is coming this way. That is no spirit. That's a man—and if we mean to escape him, we'd best go now, for he will soon be here!"

Not waiting for Hawk's reply and forgetting his concern over the problem of the Toads, Emri grabbed his bundle of possessions, shoved the cub over the lip of the rise, and leaped over the edge. In a shower of stones, he descended, bellowing noises that he hoped would sound like those of an angry spirit seeking revenge.

CHAPTER FIVE

The Toads looked up at Emri with wide eyes and open mouths, astonishment written across their flat faces, quickly followed by terror.

"*Ooo*," shrieked Emri as he waved his arms above his head and twisted his face into a number of hideous contortions. Trying to keep his balance, he plunged down the steep slope. A shower of stones rattled past him, and a demented cry echoing his own told him that Hawk had followed his example.

They quickly overtook the small boy, who threw himself off the trail, still clutching the remains of his hard-won meal in his grubby fingers. Rolling to the bottom of the incline, he leaped to his feet and scuttled away as fast as he could go.

Emri was pleased to see that the elders appeared to be just as frightened as the child. They pushed and shoved each other in a futile attempt to hide on the barren spit of land.

Emri dug his heels into the scree, slowing his descent as he reached the bottom of the trail. He put his arms out in front of him and wiggled his fingers at the frightened Toads. "Oooo," he moaned in a cracked and quavering voice. "I am the spirit of one whom you have wronged. I wander the earth in sorrow. My body lies rotting. My death was without honor. I seek those who refused me shelter before the Cold Time, those who refused me food, those who caused my death. I seek Toads. I seek *Revenge!*"

Shouting the word, Emri leaped forward and shook his fingers at the headman who had turned them away when Hawk tried to return to his tribe. The man screeched like a skewered boar and dove behind a group of women who cowered together, hiding their faces in their hands.

The group burst apart like a puddle shattered by a rock and the women ran in all directions, leaving the headman huddled on the ground alone, his thin arms wrapped over his head. There was a terrible stink as the man emptied his bowels. Emri almost felt sorry for him. Almost.

"I meant no harm," wailed the man. "I did nothing."

"That *was* the harm. You did nothing," intoned Hawk in a deep, resonant voice. "You allowed my mother to die by doing nothing, by not sharing the tribe's food. You refused us shelter and drove us away with sticks and stones when we came to you bearing gifts. Now we are here to take our revenge."

"What—what do you want?" gibbered the man, still too terrified to do more than peek at them from behind a stringy curtain of lank greasy hair.

"Your lives!" boomed Emri as he held the lion cub back with his foot to prevent Mosca from investigating this most peculiar human who was prostrating himself at cub level. This was an obvious invitation to play, from Mosca's point of view.

The headman began to wail, rocking back and forth on his knees. A few of the women began to shriek and cry and hug their children fiercely, but most stood mute, their flat faces rigid and their eyes glazed and opaque at the thought of their impending death.

"Spare me," wept the headman. "Take anything you want. Take everything we have. We will give you all we own if you spare us."

Emri glanced at Hawk, wondering what to do. Hawk nodded briefly. Emri look around at the poor pathetic Toads whose lives were scarcely more advanced than animals, and knew that they possessed little that he wanted or needed—other than the precious floating skins. But if they took less than everything, the Toads might suspect that they were not spirits after all.

"We will take your offerings," Emri said gruffly, "and spare you from our revenge."

Sobbing and wailing, the women began to heap all their meager belongings: stone knives, flat shells filled with fat and oil for lamps, sharp-edged shells and bones used for cutting and scraping, an assortment of bone fish hooks, crudely tanned skins used as blankets and carrying sacks, rough webs of woven nets, necklaces of brightly colored shells and stones, and a variety of spears whose tips had been sharpened and hardened in a slow fire. All were heaped on the ground before Emri, Hawk, and Mosca.

"Place all inside a hide," directed Emri. "Place the hide inside one of the floating skins."

The men began to mutter among themselves, their dark eyes darting furtively. The headman had scrambled to his feet and taken care to lose himself in the crowd, but this new demand brought him forward, his small eyes blinking rapidly as he steeled himself to protest.

"You cannot take the floaters. We need them to fish and place our nets. Without them we will die."

"Just as you left us to die," Hawk said coldly. You can make new floaters. It is early and Cold Time is far away. You will survive."

"Why do spirits want a floater?" shouted one of the women whose bright eyes and aggressive manner suggested one with more spirit than her companions. It was the question Emri had been dreading.

"Do you dare to question the dead?" he asked sternly, drawing himself up as tall as he could.

"We need them," replied the woman, her jaw jutting out at a stubborn angle. It was clear that, while frightened, she was determined to speak out.

"Because our hearts are large, we will take but one of the floaters," answered Emri, who was anxious to avoid a confrontation, "but you would do well to say words for us that will allow us to join our ancestors. If you do not honor us so, we will return and you will feel our true anger."

"We will say the words," the headman said quickly as he began to transfer the mound of possessions to a rumpled hide. "We will send you to the ancestors and do it well. You will have no reason to come back here again."

Emri frowned harshly and avoided looking at Hawk, knowing that he was close to laughing out loud at the success of their plan.

He looked over his shoulder at the ridge above them, anxious to be gone, fearful that the follower would arrive before they were able to make good their escape. The heaped stones that lined the peak of the ridge stood empty against the sky.

"Carry the floater up to the top of the hill," ordered Hawk. "We will take our leave of you there."

Several of the men picked up the smallest of the floaters and began walking toward the trail.

"Not that one," commanded Emri. "We will take that one," he said, pointing to the second largest.

There was a good deal of subdued grumbling, but after a moment's hesitation, the men put down the smaller vessel and picked up the one that Emri had indicated and once again retraced their steps to the foot of the trail.

"Why do spirits need a floater?" the woman with the bright eyes asked again. But no one answered her and several of her companions edged away, separating themselves from her dangerous words.

"Hurry. We would be gone," said Emri, anxious to leave before the woman stirred the Toads into some action that would result in bloodshed.

The men advanced up the trail, one in front at the head of the floater, two along the side nearest the rough wall, and another at the foot of the floater. Two others followed behind, carrying the heavy bundle that comprised all of the Toads' worldly goods. Emri, Hawk, and Mosca followed on their heels.

Then, at the last moment, Mosca turned aside, drawn by the sight and scent of the fish, still clutched in the fist of the child who had stolen it from the fisherman.

Hawk lost his grip on the cub's neck, and turned in time to see Mosca leap on the boy and grab the fish in his teeth.

The boy let out an indignant yelp and smacked the cub on the head with a closed fist. The cub yowled in anger but refused to let go. A curious tugging match ensued, complete with growling from both lion cub and child.

Emri looked back in horror, seeing his carefully constructed plan crumbling around them. Already many of the adults were looking at the cub in a puzzled manner, trying to understand why a spirit who no longer needed food would fight with a child over a scrap of raw fish.

The boy, tiring of the fight and determined not to lose his prize, seized a rock and brought it down on top of Mosca's head.

The rock caught the cub on the side of the head, just above the eye. It was a glancing blow without enough force to do any real physical damage but it was enough to break the skin, causing a slight trickle of blood to stain the chalky coating.

The Toads stared at the blood in stunned silence. One of the men carrying the bundle looked up at them, his eyes mirroring the confusion that was going on inside his head. But the outspoken woman had no such problems understanding what she was seeing.

"They are not spirits!" she exclaimed loudly, as the cub sat down on his hindquarters and pawed at his face, smearing the blood and uncovering the golden pelt that lay beneath the clay. "They are alive and have come to steal from us. Kill them!"

Emri's heart sank as comprehension crept across the vapid faces of the Toads. It appeared as though their luck had run out.

The men holding the floater lowered it slowly, their eyes cold and hard as they put the precious object down on the rough trail. Their eyes were cold and hard and the man at the foot of the vessel turned toward them, tugging at the floater impatiently, as good as telling his companions to return it to the safety of the ledge. The men carrying the bundle had already lowered it and were staring at Emri and Hawk as though waiting for further direction from someone.

"They are not spirits, they are living people. Look at them. They have covered themselves with mud. They are thieves who came to steal from us!" screamed the woman, egging on her clan. "Kill them now before they escape! Kill them! Kill them!"

The woman's shrill cries echoed in Emri's head and he knew that they were in serious trouble. The men who had carried the floater stood in front of them, between them and the top of the ridge. The men who carried the bundle stood below them on the trail. The remainder of the tribe stood on the ledge at the foot of the trail. Already many were looking around for stones. Several people, including the outspoken woman, had grabbed smoking brands from the fires and were edging closer, trying to work up the courage to attack. Emri's hand crept toward his knife and he tightened his grip around the haft of his spear. It seemed that they would have to fight their way out.

A stone arced out of the crowd and struck Emri on the chest. It was a painful blow and knocking loose the mud covering left an angry red blotch, but did no real harm. Another stone whizzed through the air and fell between Emri and Hawk. The angry Toads drew closer, those in front pushed by those in the safety of the rear. Emri knew that if the Toads were allowed to come any closer, he and Hawk would not emerge alive. He lifted his spear and poked one of the bundle carriers between the shoulder blades, hard enough to draw blood.

"We wish you no harm," he shouted. "Give us the floater and we will leave in peace. We are well armed. If we fight, many will die."

But the Toads did not seem to care. Their faces were twisted and ugly, their lips drawn back over their teeth. Stones began to fly through the air and a few struck their marks. The man standing next to Hawk at the foot of the vessel shoved Hawk hard, attempting to throw him off the trail.

Hawk staggered off balance and fell against Emri, pushing him forward. Emri's spear disappeared between the man's shoulder blades, the sharply knapped stone edges cutting through flesh and skin as easily as a stick through mud.

The Toad gave a terrible gurgling scream, threw up his arms, and hung from the end of the spear his body convulsed with spasms, wrenching it out of Emri's hands, as he collapsed on the narrow trail.

Emri gaped in disbelief as the blood gushed out of the Toad's mouth and sank into the stony soil.

Silence descended on the hostile crowd and they glared at Emri and Hawk with sullen hatred. Emri put his foot on the man's back and pulled the spear free, swallowing the nausea that rose in his throat.

He pushed the body off the trail with his foot and stared back at the crowd, his spear lifted to shoulder level, ready to throw, the point dripping with dark blood.

"Leave us alone," he repeated, "and we will go. Fight, and more will die." He stared at them, trying to force them to agree through strength of will.

It was not enough. Some lowered their eyes and looked away, but many did not.

"He killed Throm!" screamed the hated woman. "Kill them! Do not let them get away!" She pulled back her arm and hurled a rock at Emri.

Her aim was good, better than that of the men, and the rock struck Hawk on the head giving off a sound like that of a gourd when thumped to see if it were ripe. Hawk sank to his knees, his eyes rolled back in his skull, and the whites flashed as he fell forward. Emri grabbed him an instant before he toppled off the narrow ledge, but Hawk hung from his arms, dead weight threatening to pull Emri off the ledge as well. A loud squalling followed by fierce spitting filled the air and a flurry of activity divided the Toads. Emri saw Mosca surrounded by a group of children who were pummeling him with their fists, avoiding his sharp-tipped claws and angry lunges with ease. Several of the youngsters were hefting rocks and sticks like those of their elders, waiting for an opportunity to strike the clumsy cub down.

A sharp unexpected kick drove the air from Emri's lungs and he fought to keep his balance. He rolled to one side, pulling Hawk with him, struggling to free the hand that still held the spear.

The man closest to him, he who had held the skin, drew back his foot to deliver another blow and Emri knew that he would never be able to free the spear and throw it before the man knocked him from the ledge.

The man's lips were drawn back in a sneer. His eyes were bright with hatred under the black fringe of hair, chopped square above the thick line of his brows. He was so close that Emri could see where his nose had once been broken and had healed crookedly, mashed almost flat against his face so that his breath whistled with every exhalation.

Suddenly, a large stone, much larger than a man could throw, dropped on top of the Toad's head and felled him like a storm-struck tree. Air rushed out in a great sigh and he collapsed wordlessly, disappearing over the edge of the trail. Emri could only stare in perplexed amazement, wondering if the man had been struck by mistake by one of his own tribe.

But even as he wondered, other stones of equal size began to rain down from the cliff above. There was a horrible shriek and one of those who had carried the floater, fell to the ground clutching his head, which streamed with blood as it pulsed from his shattered skull. His cries soon weakened and then ceased completely, but no one paid him any heed, for the rocks continued to fall, indiscriminately striking man, woman, and child alike.

There was a sudden blur of movement as Mosca emerged from the circle of his tormentors and raced to Emri's side, almost swept from the trail as the men who had been holding the floater dropped it over the edge, as though it had no more value than a pile of worthless fish bones, and rushed down the steep ledge, attempting to escape the deadly fall of rocks. The last man, scarcely older than Emri himself, was not as fortunate as his comrades and was felled by a boulder that struck him on the nape of the neck. Emri saw the exact moment that the light of life faded from his eyes.

Emri struggled to lift Hawk, wondering if they

would be able to escape from the man who stood at the top of the ridge hurling rocks down on them.

Emri had no doubt at all as to the man's identity; he knew that it was the follower, who had caught up with them at last. The rocks were meant for them, not the Toads. The Toads had merely been unlucky enough to get in the way. He did not want to follow the Toads onto the spit of rock, but he could not stay where he was. Nor could he fight his way up the trail through the barrage of rocks carrying Hawk and hope to defend himself. Their position seemed hopeless.

Mosca whimpered as a rock bounced dangerously close to them and the last of the bearers raced by.

They were alone on the trail now, an easy target. Emri braced himself, trying to press flat against the face of the cliff so as to present as little a target as possible. Yet in his heart he knew that they would be as visible as a black bear in a snowstorm. Their death was but a matter of time.

CHAPTER SIX

"Hurry, Emri. Come up. I cannot hold them off much longer," said a hoarse whisper. Emri started as though he had been struck. Could it be that the follower was trying to help them? That voice . . . It sounded so familiar. He craned his neck forward, trying to get a glimpse of the speaker.

A dark tangled head of hair peered at him over the edge of the cliff. An electric shock coursed through his body, and mindless to the danger, he stood in the middle of the trail and stared upward. Dawn!

"Dawn! Is that you? Are . . . are you the follower?" he asked hesitantly, scarcely daring to believe what he was seeing.

"Emri, get up here! The Toads are gathering their courage. They will not stay much longer and there are few rocks left that I can move!"

Still stunned by the realization that the dread follower whom they had done their best to kill was Dawn, Emri did as he was told, slinging Hawk over his shoulder and hurrying up the incline with Mosca bounding at his heels.

Dawn was crouching behind the last of the large boulders that formed the lip of the cliff. All the smaller rocks had been dislodged to create the deadly fusillade that had driven the angry Toads away.

Emri lowered Hawk to the ground, his eyes fixed on Dawn's face. Seeing her before him did not make her presence any easier to believe.

He raised a hand and touched her face gently. He pushed the heavy tangled curls back from the beloved

43

face, feeling the grit that dulled the once-shiny hair of his dreams.

Her face bore traces of soot, the legacy of the fire, but the dark smudges that lay beneath the luminous brown eyes had been caused by exhaustion and strain, not by the fire. Her cheekbones, once as plump and colorful as the red fruit that hung from the trees in Warm Time, were sharply defined and pushed against the skin like ledges of rock.

Emri cupped her cheek in his palm, taking in the sight of her, noting the changes and wondering what had caused them. But for now, it was enough that she was there, for he had never thought to see her again.

Dawn closed her eyes. Laying her head to the side, she nestled her cheek against his hand and sighed deeply.

Emri felt a great warmth spread within his chest. It was an ache, half of sorrow, half of quiet joy. He pulled her close against him and wrapped his arms around her. Fitting her head beneath his chin, he cradled her softly without speaking, her closeness adequate without words. All else was forgotten, Toads, floater, Hawk, and even Mosca, who sat whining at his feet.

Finally, he spoke. "How come you to be here?" he asked. "How did you find us?"

He felt her stiffen, and she freed herself from his arms and stood back to look him squarely in the eye. She was calm, but he could feel the tension and the defiance that filled her.

"I am with child," she said simply, her brown eyes staring directly into his. "Mandris had not been able to force me to his bed and no other man would admit to lying with me."

"Mandris called a council of elders, and when I would not name the man I had been with, Mandris said that an evil spirit had lain with me when I slept, entering through that which makes me a woman, and got me with child. They cast me out of the tribe."

Emri stared at her, his heart sinking within his breast as he heard her words. It meant almost-certain death for a man to be cast out of the tribe, for one alone stood little chance against the animals and the elements. But a woman! Such a thing was unheard of. Emri had never known a woman to be cast out of the tribe. He could only imagine the fear that must have lived with her both day and night.

"Mandris thought that I would weep and beg him not to send me away. He thought that I would beg him to take me to his campfire. He said that I must ask his forgiveness or be gone when the sun rose from its sleep behind the blue mountains.

"He thought that I would change my mind. But I could not. He treats your mother and sisters well, but without love. I would not join his fire.

"I left before the sun wakened, taking enough food to last until I found you."

"But how did you know where to find me?" Emri asked in amazement, stunned at her courage, knowing the dangers of the land.

"Mandris told how you killed the totem," said Dawn, her eyes dropping to the ground. "He described the place where it happened. Two of the hunters, Walks Alone and Broken Tooth, were to follow one sun after I left. They are to kill you in hopes of preventing the Gods from placing a curse on the tribe."

Emri heard the words but they made no impact. Dawn's presence was all that mattered.

"And is it true?" he asked softly, holding her gaze. "Is it true about the child?"

"Yes," said Dawn, lifting her chin defiantly.

"I am glad," said Emri, and he smiled and drew her to him once more. She came willingly and fitted herself to him, seeming to grow smaller as she allowed her head and shoulders to droop.

"We must go," she said in a muffled voice. "They will not stay there forever. Even Toads can fight back."

It was hard to let go of her—the feeling of her body next to him was like a drink of water after a time of thirst—but he knew that she was right.

"Lift him carefully," said Dawn, bending to Hawk's side and brushing aside the fall of dark hair that covered the wound. "Head wounds are bad."

Holding Hawk between them, they made their way
awkwardly across the low rolling hills until they nearly
tumbled into a deep crease cut in the earth where a river
had once run. The marks of its passage were carved on
the creamy rock that lined the two sides, but the water
had changed its course and gone elsewhere, leaving the
small ravine behind. It was deep enough that even
standing upright, they could not be seen from the
surrounding land.

They lowered Hawk to the ground. A layer of soft
sand cushioned his body.

"Why does he not waken?" asked Emri, more
worried than he cared to admit. He could not bear to
think of the hard journey ahead without the companion-
ship of Hawk, whose resourcefulness and wry wit had
seen them through the hardest of times.

"Head wounds are like that sometimes," said Dawn.
"We can do nothing but make him comfortable and hope
that he will waken."

They straightened Hawk's limbs and covered him
with Emri's furskin. His skin, normally a ruddy and
weatherbeaten shade of brown, had paled to a sick
chalky color and his lips were tinged with blue. The
bruise on his head was hugely swollen, and purple-black
with blood that pooled just under the surface of the skin.

Emri sat down next to Hawk, smoothing the hair
from his brow, and drew Dawn down next to him. Mosca
licked Hawk's face and then lay down next to him,
whimpering softly.

"How did you find us?" he asked, reveling in her
nearness, yet even now scarcely able to believe that she
was really there.

"I listened carefully as Mandris told Walks Alone
and Broken Tooth where to find you. The way was clear
and easy to find. My only concern was in getting there
first and then trying to confuse the trail so that they
could not follow."

"And were you able to do this?" Emri asked,
beginning to realize the danger of her words. Walks
Alone was the best tracker and finder of game in the
Tiger clan. He found game where others found nothing.

He was a silent man who took no woman to his fire and cared little for the company of others.

"I do not think so," admitted Dawn. "Your trail was easy to follow, even for me. But the fire may well have made things more difficult for them."

"We did not think of hiding our trail until we saw you," Emri said glumly, realizing now that they should have expected such a thing. "How did you escape the fire? We might have killed you. I did not know that it was you."

"I hid in a small water place," said Dawn, resting her head on his shoulder. "The reeds burned along the edges and many animals crowded into the water with me, snakes and cats and even a small bear, but none of them paid attention to any other. They were too frightened of the fire. We stayed there until it passed us by and then we left like tribes that do not speak the same language. A spotted cat crouched at my side. It growled but it did not attempt to harm me. I see that your little one has grown."

"He has grown and learned much since we found him," said Emri, "as have Hawk and I." And during the time that followed, he told her of all that had passed since they had seen each other last. He recounted leaving the tribe and attempting to return Hawk to the Toads. Of the Toads' rejection, insisting that Hawk was a dead one, and their refusal to take him back.

He spoke of the cave they had made and told her proudly of the provisions they had gathered against the coming Cold Time. He grew excited telling of the killing of the deer, the first time he had actually killed large game.

Then came the story of their encounter with Mandris and the tiger, already debilitated with the sickness that had come from the broken fang.

His words grew slow as he spoke of the dreadful journey across the plains, pursued by Mandris and the tiger totem who were intent on their death.

He told of the terrible climb up the flank of the mountain during the first snowstorm of Cold Time. Of wandering cold and lost, and their miraculous discovery of the cave.

He told of waking to find themselves surrounded by a pride of fierce cave lions who gradually accepted their presence, and of the respect and friendship that developed between themselves and the trio of dominant lions who ruled the pride. He also spoke of the hatred of Long Tooth, a young male lion who did not share his elders' liking for the strange humans.

His voice grew thick with emotion as he recounted their descent from the mountain following the passage of Cold Time when the land was born again.

He told of the hunt and the killing of the young tusker. And he spoke of the arrival of Mandris and the tiger—now much weakened and nearly mad with pain—tied to the shaman by the herbs that dulled his agony.

His voice was flat and heavy as he told of the battle that followed. Of the deaths of Beauty and Leader and old One-Eye. He told of his reluctance to kill the tiger, the totem of his tribe, even after the tiger began to come for him. Only when Hawk had placed himself in the tiger's way, and been clubbed aside, had he struck, killing the tiger with his spear.

He told of Mandris's laughter, pleased that there was now no obstacle to prevent him from becoming the undisputed chief and shaman of the Tiger clan.

Lastly he spoke of their flight and of their plan to cross the river and seek new lands to make their home.

"It is a good plan," said Dawn as she sat up and turned to face him. "We will cross the river as you have said. There we will be safe."

Emri looked at her, his brow furrowed with concern. There was no question of sending her back; there was no longer a place for her with the Tigers. But her presence made a difficult situation even more perilous. And now there were new problems for which he had no answers.

"But, Dawn, the child. I know nothing of bringing a new one into the world. We need other women for that—and a healer, should things go wrong. Perhaps we should stay here and—"

"We will go, Emri. We will cross the river," Dawn said firmly. "There is no safety for us here."

"But how will we do it?" Emri asked, trying to reason with her. "Our plan to trick the Toads out of a floater has failed."

"Simple," said Dawn with a grin. "We'll steal it."

CHAPTER SEVEN

They remained in the dry wash until nightfall. There had been no sign of pursuit, and it soon became apparent that the Toads had decided to tend to their wounded rather than seek further confrontation. The softly rolling hills remained empty of man in all directions, for which Emri was very grateful.

All day he had kept watch, noting the passage of deer and antelope and bison who grazed on the tender new growth. Hawks, eagles, and giant condors rode the thermals high above the plains, descending occasionally in wide looping circles to swoop down on some unfortunate prey. Wings flapping awkwardly, they rose with considerably less majesty clutching their squealing target in cruel talons.

Shortly after dusk, Emri slithered over the edge of the wash and made his way toward a large mound of hard-packed dirt a short distance away. It was the den of a solitary earth digger.

Emri had watched the fat creature all afternoon as it gathered various roots, seeds, and grasses. It stuffed them into its copious cheek pouches and bore them back to its burrow, already storing foods against the next Cold Time.

Emri had admired the rich golden pelt as the animal sat in front of its burrow and groomed itself in the warmth of the setting sun. Even more, he had admired its huge belly and the thick layer of fat that covered its bones.

Moving quietly, he placed heavy rocks on all three

entrances to the burrow, the last all but concealed beneath a clump of weeds. Diligent watching had revealed all three passages as the fat earth digger had visited each during the long afternoon.

Next, Emri placed his ear flat against the ground and listened. He tuned out the murmur of wind through the grass, the sharp yipping of a coyote, and the mournful howl of a dire wolf some distance away. At first he heard nothing, and then his patience was rewarded as he caught a faint rustle of movement.

Moving carefully, Emri positioned himself above the spot where the sound was centered. He listened again, glad that Dawn was holding Mosca captive, for the hunt would be difficult enough even without the cub's dubious assistance.

Emri smiled as the sound traveled clearly through the earth. He judged the fat digger to be no more than a hand's width beneath the surface. He rose to his feet, taking great care to place his feet quietly to avoid even the slightest vibration.

Raising his spear above his head, he hesitated for a moment before plunging it deep into the earth with the full force of his body behind it. There was a brief shrill scream. He felt the earth digger jerk and kick out spasmodically, impaled on the end of his spear. He pushed hard against the spear, driving the point into the ground. The movement ceased.

Emri fell to his knees and began to dig carefully, scraping the earth away from the tunnel beneath. Soon his fingers touched the warm furry pelt of the dead digger. He pushed the earth away from the animal and then slipped his hand beneath it and pulled it from the hole.

The point of his spear had caught the creature midbody and had penetrated the lungs and the great artery. Warm blood dripped from the creature's mouth and ran down his arms as Emri raised the animal to the sky and whispered thanks to the spirits of his ancestors for guiding his spear.

Dawn received the digger with a calm assurance, as

though there had never been any doubt that Emri would return with food. Using Emri's keen-edged blade of black- and red-streaked obsidian, she separated the soft gold pelt from the carcass. Deft movements removed the organs and intestines from the interior of the creature. These she gave to Mosca along with the skull. She saved only the delicacy of the tiny liver, which she presented to Emri as his due.

Mosca swallowed the soft parts whole and then settled down to crunch upon the skull. A small slap on his nose had discouraged his interest in the bloody pelt. Dawn cut the carcass in four equal pieces, handing one section to Emri and taking another for herself.

The meat was sweet and mild with a flavor reminiscent of the plump, ground-dwelling, prairie birds that had been plentiful near the Tiger clan's camp. Emri would have preferred to roast the creature over a bed of coals but knew that such a thing would have been too dangerous. The scent of fire and roasting meat traveled far, and would betray their presence should either Toads or Tigers be searching for them.

Hawk was still lying unmoving beneath the furskin. The blood had clotted and scabbed on his head and no new blood flowed. His skin was cool to the touch, which Dawn declared to be a good sign.

When they were finished eating, they slid beneath the furskin, positioning themselves on either side of Hawk to help keep him warm during the night.

Emri pillowed his head on his arm and turned toward Dawn. Sliding his hand across Hawk's unprotesting body, he caressed her arm and rubbed her back, drawing pleasure from the feel of her. Slowly, tentatively, his hand traveled to her belly, and wordlessly, he placed his open palm against the small bulge. Dawn covered his hand with her own and smiled as she sank into sleep.

Emri wakened in the deep silence before dawn. The land was without sound, buried beneath a thick layer of white fog that drifted inland from the Endless Waters. Its damp chill lay upon his face. Mosca was rolled in a ball, huddled against Emri's side beneath the furskin. The cub had little liking for cold or moisture.

Emri reached over and shook Dawn gently. She came awake instantly.

Soon they had left the ravine and were retracing the steps they had taken the day before. Hawk had still not regained consciousness, but he stirred from time to time and muttered unintelligibly. Emri tried to believe that this was a good sign, for he could not bear to think otherwise. Already Hawk felt lighter beneath his hands, less substantial, as though part of him had already died and taken leave of his body.

Mosca objected to leaving the warmth of the furskin, and bawled and moaned in disgust. Dawn tapped him sharply on the nose each time he protested. While it did not quiet him, he soon learned to stay out of her reach.

The approach to the Toads' camp seemed clear; there was no sign of a lookout. To Emri this seemed most strange, for the Tigers would have had men posted all around the perimeter of the village had they experienced a hostile incursion. But Toads were not Tigers.

They approached the edge of the cliff carefully, in case the Toads had been clever and had set a trap. But the trail down the face of the cliff was clear and there was no sign of movement from below.

It took a few moments for their eyes to penetrate the thick fog that mingled with the smoke that rose sluggishly from the Toads' campfires.

Toads were sprawled in attitudes of sleep all over the narrow spit. A man muttered, his narrow lips twitching like a dog in the throes of a bad dream. A child whimpered and snuggled closer to his mother beneath the thin furskin that covered them both.

Emri and Dawn crept down the narrow trail, supporting Hawk's dead weight between them, the strain evident in the ache of their leg muscles. Even Mosca seemed aware of the danger and was strangely subdued. Only once did he open his mouth as though to bawl. Dawn lifted her hand and he shook his head and dodged aside, holding his silence.

They reached the foot of the trail and began to pick

their way through the tangle of sleeping Toads. There seemed to be no pattern to their positioning. It was as though they had slept wherever they last stopped. Emri could only wonder at the hopeless muddle of their lives.

They were closer to the river now. The fog was thicker, almost impossible to see through, and the sound of the river was very loud. Emri's heart began to pound, and he fought back the fear that had threatened to overwhelm him since Dawn had first outlined her bold plan. He almost envied Hawk's unconscious state. With any luck, all danger would be past by the time Hawk awakened—if he wakened.

The air was quite cold now and Emri's skin wore beads of moisture deposited by the fog. He shivered, wondering if it would have been wiser to have worn his clothing rather than carrying it wrapped in his furskin.

They drew level with the largest of the Toads' fires, which smoldered and steamed in the cold air, casting a thick pall of sullen smoke. A current of icy air gusted off the river and drove the smoke toward them, wrapping itself around their heads.

The man muttered again in his sleep and raised his hand to scratch his ear. Suddenly there was a loud sneeze! Hawk! Bleary, unfocused eyes opened and stared at the scene vaguely. A second sneeze ripped through his slender frame, and then, as though even such a slight effort were too much, his head fell forward once again and he sagged against Emri once more.

Dawn and Emri stood frozen in place, almost too terrified to look around and see if the sound had wakened anyone. But there was no movement, no cry of alarm, and slowly Emri relaxed his tensed muscles. A sneeze is a sneeze whether made by Toad or Tiger, and the sound had raised no alarms.

The remaining floaters appeared in the white mist, taking on definition as they drew closer. There were only two left, the largest and the smallest. They had passed the middle-sized floater smashed on the boulders at the side of the trail, the splintered poles sticking through the skin like a shattered bone through flesh.

They righted the larger of the two, surprised at the lightness of the thing, and as they turned it, its bottom grated harshly against the rock. They froze, but once again there was no outcry. A bird trilled, a forlorn call that echoed across the roiling whiteness that was the river. Emri could barely see the foaming brown waters that lay but a short distance away.

They lowered Hawk onto the rock, and then lifted the floater and carried it to the water's edge. There appeared to be enough space for the two of them to sit upright on the bottom and wield the long flat pieces of wood that were used to guide its passage through the water. The skins were lashed to a circle of willow in the very center.

There was adequate room both in front of and behind their seating to place their few possessions, as well as Hawk and the cub.

Emri was more than a little worried about Mosca, for there was no way to explain what was about to happen and he was uncertain of the cub's reaction. He touched the furskin that covered the fragile framework and knew how easily the cub's sharp claws could reduce it to shreds.

Dawn had evidently had similar thoughts, for she moved to Emri's side and whispered in his ear.

"We must place the cub within your furskin and give him food to quiet him. We will secure him so he cannot cut the skins. He will not like it, but it must be done."

Emri nodded, knowing that she was right but already anticipating the cub's angry protests.

They loaded Dawn's small bundle into the front end and placed Hawk's possessions in the rear, saving his furskin to spread along the bottom. They placed Hawk atop the furskin, arranging him as comfortably as possible. Emri wished that Hawk were awake to help them with his knowledge of how to handle the strange floater.

Taking a deep breath, Emri grabbed Mosca and stuffed him and one of the two remaining pieces of the digger inside the heavy outer covering he had worn through the Cold Time. It was made of deerskin and lined with rabbit fur. Working quickly, before Mosca realized what was happening and fought back, Emri drew the drawstrings tight at the waist and the neck and tied the arms together around the cub's body. Mosca bawled loudly and struggled against the heavy folds. Emri grimaced, remembering all of the hard work that had gone into the garment's construction and hoping that the cub did not destroy it before they were able to set him free.

Placing the squirming bundle next to Hawk, Dawn and Emri lifted the floater which was now much heavier and staggered with it to the very edge of the water.

Emri gestured at Dawn to get in. She had just settled herself, picking up the length of wood, when a shadowy figure appeared almost beside her.

A Toad, his eyes still gummy with sleep, stood with mouth agape holding his genitals in his hand, his skinny naked flanks covered with cold-bumps. He stared at them without comprehension for a long disbelieving moment. Then Emri saw the sharp light of understanding come to him, and the man's eyes narrowed even as his mouth opened to shout.

He never got the chance. Lifting the length of the wood used to steer the floater, Emri slammed it against the side of the man's head. The man made a small choking sound and fell sideways into the river, which curled around his body, rolling him over once as though tasting him, and then swallowed him whole.

Dawn stared at Emri with stricken eyes, holding onto the willow binding with whitened fingers.

Emri did not speak; there was nothing to say. Had he not silenced the man, his cries would have brought every Toad in the camp down on them before they could escape.

The moment was upon them; there was no turning back. He seized the willow framework and lifted the floater into the water, holding firm against the furious tug of the current and hoping that it would indeed float— although in his heart he could not imagine such a thing.

Then, uttering prayers to his ancestors, he leaped into the floater in one swift motion. Instantly, they were seized by the current and flung headlong into the grip of the maelstrom. The fog closed in upon them, and within the blink of an eye they were out of sight of the land.

CHAPTER EIGHT

The current threw them back and forth, hurling them as easily as a child playing with a throwing stone. The water rose up in frightening peaks on either side of them, snarling and hissing as though it were angry that they dared to ride on its back.

Emri did his best to guide the floater with the flat stick, but it did little good and the rapid current threatened to pull it from his hands. Already Dawn had seen the futility of such actions, and had drawn the stick inside and braced herself against the willow framework to prevent being thrown out of the floater.

Its wild gyrations made such a thing entirely possible and Emri fought a surge of fear and nausea as the floater whirled about in a circle, caught in a confluence of conflicting currents.

A huge floating tree twice the height of their heads rushed at them, appearing out of nowhere, seemingly bent on their destruction. At the last instant, Emri fended it off with his stick, pushing the floater away and freeing it from the circle of currents as well.

The fog was still thick, although here and there it was torn by gusts of wind, providing them with even more frightening glimpses of the brown torrent. The banks were not visible; all that could be seen was water, water, and more water.

Rocks poked through the water periodically, like teeth waiting to gash the floater open or chew them up and spit out their remains. Emri and Dawn used their sticks as best they were able to keep the floater off the rocks. But there were other dangers as well.

Trees, many as large as the first, sped by, tumbling over and over in the flood. The branches were the danger, each one capable of tipping the floater and dragging them beneath the surface of the water. They hacked and slashed at the branches and plunged their sticks deep into the water, clawing for purchase. Remarkably, this tactic seemed to work, and they quickly realized that the depth of the sticks was crucial for any measure of control over the floater.

The floater itself was as treacherous as any of the obstacles, always attempting to turn on its side. They learned that balance was everything and that they had to distribute their weight as evenly as possible over the center pole. If one leaned to the side, it was mandatory for the other to remain upright, as both leaning too far to one side threatened to overturn the floater completely.

Nothing had been heard from Hawk or Mosca, and Emri had little time to spare them thought. It was possible that the cub was silent from fear, for the current could be clearly felt through the bottom of the floater. At times it seemed that there was nothing between them and the water. More than once, Emri had felt some unknown object bump and scrape along the bottom of the floater and he had been fearful that it would rip the fragile skin apart. Somehow, it had not happened.

The air grew brighter, glistening and shining around them, and it almost seemed that they could see each individual drop of water as it hung in the air. Miraculously, the fog began to dissipate, breaking up into thin tendrils that were blown apart by the wind.

Then, suddenly, it was gone, and though the river flowed no less rapidly and the danger was just as great, their spirits lightened and the fear lifted from their hearts.

The river was wide, flowing between the two distant banks. It was this very width, allowing the water to spread out, no longer locked between rigid banks, that finally stilled the awful turbulence. At last the floater came to an almost total stop, floating lightly in place atop the brown swells.

Dawn and Emri rested against the willow framework, their arms feeling as though they were weighted with stones and their shoulders, necks and lower backs burning with the pain of muscles called upon to do work other than their norm. As their breath came easier, they raised their heads and looked around in wonder.

Behind them the fog still filled the channel of the river as it flowed between the banks. The fog was dark and threatening, and Emri was glad that they had left it behind.

In front of them and to either side was water. The sun shone brightly, reflecting off the thick brown water in white spots so bright it hurt their eyes. The land was a dark smudge on either side, distant but comforting to see.

Ahead of them there was nothing but water, the brown of the river already diluted and marked with streaks of greenish blue. Emri wondered if they were near the edge of the Endless Waters. Above them, white birds wheeled and soared, their harsh thin cries echoing in the empty sky as though seeking an answer to some unspoken question.

"This is where the God of the Endless Waters makes his home," said Emri. "Hawk told me that He is near here. I think that it must be so, for I can smell His scent."

Dawn lifted her head and inhaled deeply, grimacing at the heavy salty tang of dead fish that hung on the air. Just then, the floater lifted; gently it rose and then lowered. At first, Emri thought that some submerged object had passed beneath them causing the floater to rise, but there had been no bump, no feel of anything solid. Then, just as he began to feel relieved, it happened again. Emri and Dawn looked at each other in alarm.

"Look, Emri," said Dawn as she pointed outward toward the distant watery horizon. "The water comes in soft bumps. What makes it so? Are there long animals or giant snakes beneath the surface that we cannot see?"

"Perhaps it is the God of the Endless Waters," Emri

said in a low voice as the floater lifted and rode the crest of yet another soft swell.

"I think it is the breath of the God," said Dawn. "See how it comes with spaces in between each rise. I believe it is His breath."

"Will He not mind our presence?" Emri asked, looking about him fearfully. His only experience with water was the placid stream that flowed past the Tiger camp. Even his feet had never been far from the solid sand bottom. The level had never been higher than his waist and the banks had always been within reach. Once, he and Hawk had fallen into a storm-swollen stream much, much smaller than this one and it had very nearly taken their lives. Not only was Emri frightened of the circumstances in which they had placed themselves, but he was also very concerned with angering a God with whom he was totally unfamiliar.

"It does not appear that we have offended Him," replied Dawn, lifting her face to the welcome warmth of the sun. "He has had time to eat us if that is what He wanted. Perhaps we are too little for Him to notice, for He is very, very large. Such a God would not bother Himself with us. We would be no more than a beetle on His littlest finger."

"It could be that you are right," said Emri, sensing the wisdom of her words. "But I would feel better with my feet on the ground. Let us see if we can persuade the floater to bring us to land."

It was easer said than done. Even though they had learned the trick of biting deep into the water with their sticks, the floater was stubborn and resisted their efforts, more often standing in place or drifting sideways than moving toward land.

Only after the sun had climbed to the highest point in the sky before it began its descent did they discover that Dawn, seated in the rear, could use her stick to direct their course. Plunging her stick deep into the water deeply caused the floater to turn about completely in a tight circle. Placing it in less than halfway caused it to turn again, yet more slowly. Dipping it in only a short distance on one side would cause the floater to go in the opposite direction. They found that they could go straight if Emri paddled on the side of the floater opposite from Dawn's stick. Somehow their efforts drove them straight ahead and prevented them from turning in either direction.

In spite of their discoveries, they were being carried toward the Endless Waters by the persistent current, which was far stronger than they. It was hard to keep up the steady strokes needed to drive them forward, and now the sun, which had been so welcome after the cold fog, burned down on their heads and shoulders with a ruthless intensity. Too late they realized that they had not thought to fill their waterskins. Worse, the water around them was brackish and heavy with salt which cracked their lips, twisted their bellies with knots of pain, and increased their thirst cruelly.

Hawk still lay on the bottom of the floater, muttering occasionally and once in a great while lifting an arm or a leg, but mostly he was quiet.

The same could not be said for Mosca.

Although initially quiet, the cub had soon begun to protest his confinement, twisting and struggling inside the heavy garment while growling and moaning his displeasure. At one point, fearing that the cub's violent thrashings would cause the floater to tip, Emri had placed his foot on the hide bundle. Instantly, fiery pricks of pain lanced into his foot and he kicked out, hard, banging the bundle against the wooden framework. The cub had yowled loudly, his angry screams scarcely able to be heard over the violence of the water, and after a number of convulsive spasms, he had fallen silent.

Emri was almost afraid to open the bundle, not knowing what he might find. It was possible that he had injured the cub, so hard had he kicked him. It seemed that it would be some time before they reached land, and there could not be much air inside the garment.

Drawing the heavy skin toward him by the sleeve, Emri was reassured to hear a low "*waao*" emanating from the bundle. Dawn rested on the framework as Emri cautiously opened the bundle and looked inside.

Two baleful gold eyes glared back at him, and then

the cub pushed his head out of the skin and struggled to bring his front paws forward. Emri seized the cub's paws through the deerskin and held on hard, gripping the hind legs between his thighs as they sought purchase.

"Quick, Dawn, pull the drawstring tight around his neck. We can't risk letting him get his feet out," shouted Emri. "One swipe with those claws and he'll lay the whole thing open!"

Dawn was quick to obey him. Even so, they had several nasty moments as the floater rocked back and forth violently, threatening to spill them into the brown water.

Finally the cub was subdued, tied securely with only his head protruding from the bundle. He moaned and yowled his angry protests but did not succeed in freeing himself. He struggled a while longer, thrashing back and forth across the narrow bottom of the floater, but he soon realized that his efforts were futile, and ceased, contenting himself with furious looks and harsh, open-mouthed panting.

"I feel bad for him," said Emri. "He has no way of understanding what is happening."

"It would be better if you felt bad for us," said Dawn as she wearily pushed herself upright and picked up the stick again. "We are moving quickly toward the Endless Waters. I cannot see the land now and I fear being lost on this broad water."

Emri shifted his gaze from Mosca and saw that Dawn had spoken truly. The land was but a dull mark on either side, and the color of the water was now more greenish blue than brown.

Emri picked up his stick and dug it into the water, feeling the stiff resistance of the undercurrent tug at the submerged wood. And now, for the first time, he heard something else, a dull constant throbbing roar as though someone were beating on a hollow log with a stick. He could not imagine what the noise could mean unless it was the sound of the Water God himself. Emri felt a hollowness in the pit of his stomach as fear began to gnaw at his entrails.

CHAPTER NINE

The man dropped to his knees and, placing his face level with the ground, studied the print stamped in the soft earth. His black eyes took in every detail, missing nothing.

He observed the edges of the print, noting the slightly drier tiny particles of earth that had crumbled around the edges telling him the length of time since his prey had passed. He noted the depth of the print, which told him whether his quarry had added anything to the burden he bore. Lastly, he studied the depth of the imprint left by the ball of the foot to see how fast his prey had been traveling.

When the earth could tell him no more, he rose and, without even a glance at his companion, set off at a trot, anxious to make up for lost time.

It had been a clever ploy, the fire. Walks Alone had no doubt that it had been set by Emri and the Toad in an attempt to kill them. In this they had failed. Walks Alone's lip curled in a snarl of contempt that was as close as he could come to an open display of humor. It would take far more than a fire to remove him from the hunt. The fire had been but a brief inconvenience, nothing more. He and Broken Tooth had sustained a few burns on feet and legs which would soon heal, in spite of his companion's grimaces of pain and suggestions that they return to camp. Pah! Broken Tooth was a whiner. Walks Alone ignored him. Let him do as he wished. Go or return; it meant nothing to him. He, Walks Alone, would follow the trail and kill Emri and the Toad; they who had dared to slay the totem and threatened to bring the anger of the Gods down on the entire tribe. Walks Alone would see them dead, or die in the trying.

They had run before the fire and had found shelter in a small stream that meandered across the plains. The fire had also provided them with food in the form of a slow moving horny-back who had been unlucky enough to tip on its back and had not risen. Walks Alone had scraped aside the burned hair and top layer of blackened flesh and eaten his fill of the rich meat and sweet fat. When his belly could hold no more, he had laid the segmented shell aside, leaving the remainder to Broken Tooth, tired of listening to the man's endless complaints.

The scorched earth was still hot, but their heavily callused feet were accustomed to discomfort. They continued following the tracks of the two men and the cat, leaving the burned lands behind them and entering the sandy grasslands as they approached toward the river.

But now there was a new element. Walks Alone was startled to see that a third set of prints had intersected those of Emri and the Toad. He studied them intently, absorbing information as easily as another man might learn by looking at a face.

This new person was small and light, no larger than the Toad. Yet they traveled slower and were more heavily burdened. Here the weight was placed on the heel, indicating a heavy backpack, yet there the weight of the body was pressed down solidly on the ball of the foot, indicating some additional weight well centered. A heavy person would leave such a mark, but the size and width of the print told Walks Alone that the person was small, perhaps even a woman.

Walks Alone rejected this thought almost immediately. No woman would walk by herself without the protection of a tribe or at least a man by her side. No, there must be some other answer that he had not yet discerned.

Walks Alone rose and began following the new

tracks, knowing that sooner or later he would solve the
puzzle. He knew that it was merely a matter of time
before he caught up with those he pursued. And when
he did, he would kill them.

CHAPTER TEN

The booming noise was louder now, so loud that it was hard to talk, even if they had had the energy. The sound seemed to penetrate the stillness that held Hawk captive, and he moved restlessly on the floor of the floater, rolling his head from side to side and waving his hands and legs weakly. While Emri took this activity as a good sign, the additional movement made the floater even more unstable and affected their progress.

Mosca's earlier growls and hisses had ceased. Now the cat was clearly frightened. He lay still in his confinement, no longer struggling, his ears flattened against his skull and the pupils of his gold eyes greatly dilated. He panted loudly, and spittle saturated his throat and drooled from his chin.

The waters no longer fought among themselves. The God of the Endless Waters was the clear victor.

They had lost all hope of gaining the far bank. Remaining upright quickly became their prime concern. For as the incoming waves met the current flowing downriver, the water heaved and jumped and sometimes smashed together throwing itself upward in a huge plume of froth. Even one such wave would easily smash their floater into small bits.

It was clear that they were being swept down into the vast emptiness with every passing breath and that their efforts were all but futile against the awesome power of the current.

Emri, seated in the prow, abandoned his efforts to reach the far bank, and pointing the floater downstream tried to avoid the worst of the turbulence. The water boiled on either side and an immense log swept past them before they had even noted its existence. Although untouched by the log, the danger it presented left them shaken. Shouting to be heard over the noise of the water, Emri charged Dawn with the responsibility of watching the rear as well as paddling.

The dreadful booming sound grew louder and louder. It echoed in their skulls and wore on their nerves. Emri tried to imagine what the God who made such a sound would look like. Perhaps there would be a way of avoiding the death that awaited them if he could only envision what the God looked like.

If the booming sound was the God's breathing, what was the hissing sound that underlay the heavier noise? Emri could only picture a great mouth, large enough to swallow them whole as well as huge trees and other hapless victims of the flood. Try as he might, he could not envision a face. Perhaps that was all there was, just a huge gaping mouth that everything was swept into and swallowed whole. It was a terrifying thought and one that he did not share with Dawn. He wondered why Hawk had not mentioned such a thing, and then decided that his friend had tried to spare him the fright of such knowledge.

They crested a great swell, and as they did so, Emri felt something rub against his leg as it swept along the bottom of the floater. It was an eerie sensation. At first he thought that it was but a submerged log, but then the thing, whatever it was, brushed against him again coming from the opposite direction.

Emri sat stock still, frozen with shock, wondering if the God were reaching up for him, ready to pluck him out of the water, too hungry to wait for him to be swept into its mouth.

Then he saw it, and frightened as he was, he was relieved to know that it was not the Water God after all, merely the thing that Hawk had called a biter.

A short distance away, no more than a man's length, a great upright fin broke the water and then disappeared in a trail of white foam, and Emri felt the thing's tentative touch once more. Dawn screamed shrilly and the harsh grating sensation was transmitted through the fragile skin of the floater as the frightening creature scraped along the length of the craft.

It surfaced alongside them, longer than the entire floater. It cut through the water easily, seemingly untroubled by the force of the current. A single large black eye stared at them blankly, the great mouth gaped wide, filled with row after row of sharp-pointed teeth that could cut them in half without trying. Then it was gone, disappearing as quickly as it had come, into the depths of the dark water.

There was no time for fear or for the immense relief that followed, for the water was growing ever more turbulent. It tossed them from side to side as converging currents slammed into them from all directions.

The *boom-hiss-boom-hiss* had grown still louder, and as they crested the top of an exceptionally high wave, Emri saw the reason at last. The mouth of the river was within sight, a narrowed place squeezed between two headlands of rock as the land curved in on either side like the pincers of a beetle. And sprinkled between them like the teeth of an old woman were a large number of tall rocks.

Emri waited until they were lifted by another wave, and then studied the rocks to see if there might be a path of safety between them.

It was a frightening situation. The headlands appeared to be without beaches on which they might land. The water foamed and crashed against the steep walls, which rose straight to the plateaus above without break. Even if they could land, they could not climb.

The rocks were even worse. The waves rolling in from the Endless Waters hurled themselves at the rocks in an endless progression of foam-tipped breakers. The rocks were black and shiny, dripping with water and water-weed. They gleamed in the bright sunlight, the sun reflecting off their wet surfaces as the water cascaded down the sides of the rocks in foaming torrents.

The awful booming noise that had so terrified them was produced by the waves striking the headland and

the rocks with incredible force. The hissing was the
result of the receding waves as they withdrew reluctantly while gathering themselves for yet another assault.

Emri could see no sign of the Water God, but
neither could he see any way through the teeth of the
passage. For the rocks were positioned not in a straight
line, but unevenly, some close together, some stacked
behind one another so that there was no one clear
opening. As he watched, the log that had so nearly
struck them was drawn into the maelstrom.

At first it seemed that it would pass between two
jagged rocks, the very two that Emri had noted, thinking
that they presented the widest, safest-looking space. But
then, for no reason that Emri could discern, the log
turned broadside and slammed into the rocks. Then,
incredibly, it was sucked down beneath the water until it
vanished completely!

As Emri stared in open-mouthed astonishment, the
log shot up out of the water a man's length away from the
spot it had disappeared and was flung onto the rocks
once again. Emri and Dawn backpaddled furiously as
they watched the log smash against the rock, disappear
beneath the waves, and then reemerge only to begin the
sequence again.

They did not stay to watch the final demise of the
log. Each time it crashed against the rocks, some portion
of it was whittled away. It was obvious that it would
remain either until it became small enough to escape the
deadly game or until it disappeared completely, battered
beyond recognition. It was also obvious that such would
be their fate unless they were able to devise some plan to
avoid the pull of the current around the rocks.

Even more crucial was the timing. It was necessary
that they do this soon, before they were too exhausted.
Emri felt the burning ache deep in his muscles. As one
well acquainted with the needs and messages of his
body, Emri knew that this burning signaled the edge of
his physical strength. If he were to push much further,
his exhausted body would attempt to respond but would
find muscles that trembled and shook with fatigue and
had no strength to perform the required tasks. If they

were to find a way through the rocks, it would have to be soon.

"Emri, look!" cried Dawn, leaning over his shoulder and speaking directly into his ear. He followed her pointing finger and saw what he had not noticed before. To the left, in the opposite direction they hoped to go, quite close to the headland, was a straight race of water that poured between two tall spires of rock and shot out the far side. There was no ebb and flow, and no deadly suction of the sort that pulled the log under. In fact, it almost seemed too smooth, the water a continuous gout forced between the twin spires.

Emri eyed the rocks nervously, wondering if the space between them were too narrow for the floater. They would have to position the floater precisely if they were to pass through safely. Too far to either side and they would crash upon the rocks. If they passed too far to the left, the current would seize them and fling them against the headland where they and the floater would be ground to bits.

Emri dug his stick into the water, fighting hard to get them where they wanted to go, struggling against the pull of the current with every bit of strength that remained. He felt Dawn breathing hard against his back as she did her best to keep up with him. Emri could only guess at how she must feel. He felt a deep pang of remorse but fought it down, knowing that he must concentrate completely on the task before him. Later, if they survived, there would be time for comfort.

Incredibly, the place was drawing near. Their desperate efforts had brought them close enough to see their intended passage clearly. Viewed closely it was even more frightening than from afar. Now it was possible to see why the water ran so smooth. Close under the surface lay a ledge over which the water flowed swiftly, creating a springboard for the torrent as it flowed between the rocks.

The rocks themselves were more closely positioned than Emri had first thought, and were edged with numerous jagged and sharp projections, each capable of slicing through the thin skin of the floater.

Emri's heart faltered and he could feel his muscles trembling. His throat ached as he attempted to swallow.

But there was nothing to be gained by waiting. Digging his stick into the water he guided the floater closer to the ledge. As they drew near, the far edge of the current caught them, and only then did he realize just how fast the water was running. The smoothness of the flow was deceptive, and the stick was all but wrenched from his hands as he tried to pull them closer using the ledge itself as a stabilizer.

Anchored by the stick, the floater spun around, flung out of control by the force of the water. The current seized the floater and for a moment they whirled away, spinning in circles. The rocks rushed toward them and only with the very greatest of efforts were they able to break free of the current and drag themselves back to the spot where they had begun.

This time Emri was most careful not to draw too close to the ledge. Backpaddling, they fought the onrushing water until they were positioned head-on, centered in front of the ledge. Emri held them in place with the very last of his strength, concentrating, waiting for the right moment.

It came at last, a great downpouring of water, a great wave that flung itself headlong at the rocks. Emri screamed *"Now!"* and dug into the water with his stick, propelling them into the center of the wave, straightening the floater and directing it into the space between the two rocks. He judged that the great wave would carry them safely over the ledge and between the twin spires.

The speed was exhilarating. In spite of his fear, Emri felt his heart soar as the great wave picked them up and carried them over the ledge. He felt the bottom touch and scrape once and then they were up, over, and through the rocks. He felt their dark shadow pass over his body, saw the shell-encrusted black rock out of the corner of his eye. Then they were dumped with a jarring shock on the far side.

Almost before they could catch their breath, another rush of water showered down on them, inundating them and pouring into the floater. Dawn and Emri gasped with shock as the cold water cascaded over their bodies and they paddled furiously.

And then, suddenly it was over. The floater rode peacefully on the surface of the water, rising and falling gently atop the smooth fat swells. The turbulence fell swiftly behind them as they were drawn rapidly out onto the empty vista of the Endless Waters.

"Is it over?" Dawn asked tremulously. "What now?"

"I do not know," Emri said wearily, leaning on the edge of the willow framework. "I cannot think, I cannot plan. My thoughts are too tired to come. For now, it is enough that we are alive."

He twisted as far as the floater would allow and placed his arm around Dawn's shoulders. His arm was heavy and felt as though someone had tied rocks to it. But Dawn was warm and comforting and being near her was good.

They rested for some time and then checked on their charges. Hawk was still again, lying half awash in a puddle of seawater. But he did not seem any worse than he had been.

Mosca seemed to be in shock. His eyes were glazed and, although open and staring, seemed to see nothing. His limbs were stiff yet his body was warm. Rousing him would serve no good purpose, as they could not free him from his confinement. Making certain that his head remained out of the water, they left him to recover at his own pace.

The sun was going down, descending into the Endless Waters. The clouds, hanging heavily over the water, were suffused with scarlet and gold, and the water itself shone with a brilliant gold incandescence. Each swell, each wave, was tipped with a fiery golden light. They themselves were washed with streamers of radiance. They gazed at each other with silent wonder and watched as the great glowing ball disappeared over the edge of the world and disappeared from sight, leaving them in darkness.

CHAPTER ELEVEN

Emri had experienced both cold and hunger in his lifetime, but having grown up next to a river, thirst was all but unknown. Never had he lacked for adequate drinking water. Now, as his lips cracked and his tongue grew thick, the sight of the vast quantities of undrinkable water that surrounded them was a cruel torment.

They dozed fitfully through the long night, each taking their turn at watching the dark heaving waves, for they were frightened of the nameless life-forms that filled the waters beneath them. Little could be seen—what they could see, they did not recognize. But the darkness was filled with strange watery snorts, high-pitched squeaks, large bulging eyes that cruised alongside examining them curiously, and tall fins trailing wakes that glowed like green fire.

They met the cold dawn almost more exhausted than they had been at nightfall. It was with a great sense of relief that Emri sighted a long finger of sand that thrust itself out from the land, wrapped in the cold white mists of morning.

They had no problem landing the floater, despite the fact that a large stream exited the land a short distance from the narrow spit.

The floater drifted in effortlessly and ground to a halt in the firm sand at the water's edge. For a long heartbeat, Emri stared listlessly at the beach, almost too exhausted to comprehend that they had actually returned to land alive.

His lower body was stiff almost to the point of

immobility and the cold water had leached all warmth and all feeling from his legs—except that of pain.

Dawn was in little better condition. Her lips and fingers were blue with cold, and deep grooves of exhaustion bracketed her mouth. She stumbled as she attempted to climb out of the floater. The craft tipped to the side, throwing Dawn and Emri into the foaming water.

Shocked by the cold water, Emri scrambled to his feet. Dawn crawled onto the beach and lay there, outstretched, fingers gripping the sand tightly as though she would never let go.

Moving slowly, Emri pulled the floater high up onto the beach until it wedged firmly in the dry sand above the broken bits of detritus that marked the water's highest march. Then he removed Mosca and, releasing him from his confinement, set him loose on the sand. The cat had soiled himself, and his throat and chest were matted with spittle and seawater. For a long moment, he lay unmoving on the sand, then, as Emri turned back to retrieve Hawk, Mosca sat up slowly, looked around with a vague expression, and shook his head.

Emri's heart lifted with the cat's movement. Mosca would be all right. He was less certain about Hawk. Hawk still lay motionless, his always-thin features taking on the shape of the bone beneath them, the skin pale with a tinge of blue around the nose and mouth. It seemed to Emri that Hawk breathed too slowly and too seldom, as though his spirit were preparing to leave the body that had been its home.

Shelter would have to be arranged for Hawk as well as for themselves. Grateful as Emri was for the appearance of the spit of land, it was too open, too exposed to the steady cold wind that blew off the Endless Waters. And now that he knew something of the creatures that lurked beneath its surface, he was afraid of remaining near the water's edge. Somehow, he must move them all to higher land and find some form of shelter where they might be warm and safe.

Emri squatted in the sand and laid his hand on

Dawn's shoulder, grimacing in agony as a starburst of white lights pricked at his numbed limbs.

Dawn stirred beneath his touch and sat up slowly, pushing long wet strands of hair back from her face.

"We must find shelter," Emri said through stiff, salt-rimmed lips. "Our brother's spirit is trying to leave his body. We must do what we can to persuade it to stay."

Dawn did not reply, merely nodded and, rolling onto her knees, pulled herself to her feet with Emri's assistance. She placed both of her hands in the small of her back and stretched carefully with obvious pain, the roundness of her belly prominent against her thin, wet garment.

Together, they carried Hawk's body, bowing under its light weight. Their feet found no even purchase in the slippery sand and they staggered toward the land that beckoned to them with the promise of familiar things.

At length, as their breath rasped in their throats and their limbs trembled with exhaustion, they clambered slowly across an immense deadfall of storm-tossed trees and rocks, skirted a pool of quiet water, and passed under the first of the great trees.

Leaving Dawn and Hawk at the foot of a tree, Emri went on alone to find a location better suited to their needs. He found such a place close to the edge of the stream. Unlike the Toads' river, this stream was placid and slow-moving, and Emri was able to see through the clear water to the bottom, assuring himself that it was too shallow to harbor any of the monsters that inhabited the Endless Waters.

He found the shelter he had been searching for in the shape of two large trees that had fallen in some long forgotten storm and lay wedged together close to the ground. The underbrush had sprung up around them, reaching for the spot of light torn in the dense canopy above by the death of the larger trees. Still young and flexible, it was possible to bend and weave the ambitious saplings into the tangled mass of fallen trees and branches forming a roof that would allow for the passage of air and smoke, yet keep out the worst of the weather.

He half carried Dawn to the shelter, with Mosca

following at his heels, then settled her within the rude shelter before returning for Hawk. A third trip was made to the floater, with leaden limbs, where he retrieved their possessions and dragged them back to the shelter.

Dawn had recovered sufficiently to clear out some of the debris that littered the underside of the fallen trees, and had begun to assemble bits of deadwood for a fire.

Hawk and their few belongings were carried inside the shelter, but any hopes they might have had for a quick fire were dashed, for the fire coal sheltered in its tightly sealed clam shell had burned itself into a pile of black ash. Forcing his aching limbs to perform one final task, Emri picked up his fire sticks, a straight slender bit of hardwood and another flat length and began the tedious job of continuous twirling that would eventually result in a tiny ember of fire.

The dampness of the woods so near to the water, as well as the heavy mist that pervaded even their small shelter, made his task more difficult, and only when sweat stung his eyes and his hands and arms hung heavy from his shoulders was he rewarded by the tiniest glow of orange.

Dawn was ready. Cheek to the ground, a hand's span from the small spark, she blew gently on the twirling point until the spark grew in size and brightness, then she carefully sprinkled a pinch of silky milkweed down along its edges where the infant fire could feed.

She held her breath, watching to see if the fire would catch, for it was at this crucial moment that a fire most often died. Happily, this was not such a time and the tiny spark fed greedily on the food she had provided. Anticipating its needs, she added a sprinkling of finely powdered dry wood and then, as it grew, tiny twigs and, finally, whole limbs.

Emri stacked the wood they had gathered against the fire in such a manner that the fire would continue to burn untended for a time. Dawn spread their sleeping fur out on the ground and Hawk was placed in the center so that again he might share their warmth. Emri and

Dawn lay down on either side of his still form and covered themselves with a second skin, fur side in.

Sleep was not long in coming, even though their bellies rumbled with hunger and their bodies ached and trembled with pain. They were alive, they were safe, they were together, and for the time, that was enough.

They looked at each other in the rosy glow of the firelight and smiled. Their arms twined across Hawk's thin chest, and as Mosca thrust his way under the skin and curled up in the hollow behind Emri's knees, they slept.

CHAPTER TWELVE

Walks Alone and Broken Tooth were moving swiftly now, Emri and Hawk's trail easy to follow in the soft earth. They had gained no further information about the third person, but it was of no importance. Walks Alone knew that when the time came, he would slay them all. By casting his lot with Emri and the Toad, the newcomer had chosen death.

Broken Tooth and Walks Alone studied the Toad camp from behind the few boulders that still remained at the top of the ridge. It was not difficult to piece together what had happened. What was puzzling, however, was the fact that it had happened at all. Why, wondered Walks Alone, why would the Toad attack his own people?

The camp had been hit hard. Many Toads had been killed outright by the boulders or had been gravely injured.

As Walks Alone pondered the scene, Broken Tooth gave a sudden gasp and clutched Walks Alone's bicep. Following his companion's pointing finger, Walks Alone saw a small group of people, two men, three women, and a child, sitting quietly around a smoking fire. The woman was turning the meat, which had been placed directly upon the coals, with a forked stick.

Walks Alone shook his head, seeing nothing of importance, and had turned to snarl at Broken Tooth when something about the scene caught at his mind. He turned back and studied the group more closely. Suddenly he felt the gag of sickness fill his throat as he recognized an arm and other portions of human anatomy roasting in the smoky fire, confirming the rumors he had heard all his life. Eaters of the dead! Chills ran down Walks Alone's back as Broken Tooth retched in the stones behind them.

To suffer such a fate was all but unthinkable; Walks Alone's mind reeled at the thought. One's spirit could never join the ancestors and would never light a campfire in the night sky to shine down on the living, giving them hope and comforting their sorrow. One's spirit would wander the earth, forever outcast.

Walks Alone looked around him fearfully, more than half expecting to see the spirits of the dead. Though he saw nothing, he was not reassured.

Fear prickled down Walks Alone's back. It was not safe to stay in this place of evil. While afraid of little that was alive, save the largest of beasts, Walks Alone had an absolute terror of the unknown—and especially of spirits. It was well-known that a vengeful spirit could kill a man as easily as a spearpoint. Yet it was necessary to know what had happened. Steeling himself to face the unknown, he felt a cold rage fill him, a hatred for the Toads and their primitive ways.

Signaling Broken Tooth to follow him, Walks Alone clutched his spear and his club and strode down the steep incline, entering what remained of the Toad camp.

His loud shouts brought those who were still able to rise to their feet, groping for their crude weapons, but the fight was gone from them, driven out by the previous day's destruction. Most—men as well as women and children—ran screaming from these new attackers, hiding behind boulders, rocks, any semblance of shelter. There they cowered, holding their heads and crying aloud.

Some few stood their ground, and these were killed by Broken Tooth and Walks Alone without hesitation. For despite his gentle nature, Broken Tooth held no love for Toads, regarding them as less than human. He swung his club relentlessly, as though killing the Toads might expunge the sight of roasting human flesh. He felt as well as heard the crack of a skull as it shattered beneath his club, and dodged a blow from a woman who swung a length of firewood at him. Without thinking, he brought his club down and her features were obliterated. Drenched by her hot blood, Broken Tooth was overcome by a mixture of rage, fear, hatred, and loathing. He held his own alongside his fierce clansman, and when at last they stopped, only a few small children remained alive.

Broken Tooth sank down onto a low rock and rested his forehead on the base of his club, dimly noting that his hands and arms and even his chest were splattered with blood and other bits of gore. His breath rasped harshly in his throat and his chest ached as though it were being squeezed by giant hands. He struggled to bring himself under control. Never before had he done such a thing.

He had fought men when a hunting party had come into conflict with another clan over territory, but that had involved mostly yelling and shouting of insults and waving of spears. Blows had been traded, but no actual blood had been shed. Never had he killed another man, and never women and children.

He tried to tell himself that they were but Toads and did not matter, but, still, his mind was uneasy. He vowed to say the words that would send the spirits on the way to their ancestors at the first opportunity. But he would do so without telling Walks Alone.

Normally slow to act and given to much thought, Broken Tooth was no fool. He was well aware of Walks Alone's opinion of him, and while he did not care enough to alter his actions, he saw no reason to anger the man outright.

Walks Alone, equally bloodied, had needed no time to gather his thoughts, his mind appeased, rather than disturbed, by the carnage. As Broken Tooth joined him, he grabbed the lone adult survivor, an ancient potbellied crone with hair as white as the snows and rheumy eyes caked with pus, and attempted to speak to her despite the constant monotone screech that issued from her lips.

Walks Alone shook the woman hard enough to snap her head back on her thin neck.

"Stop your noise and speak true words and perhaps I will allow you to live," he said in a harsh tone, and the noise trailed off to a weak whine.

"You were attacked by a Toad and a man of the Tiger clan," he said tersely. The woman gibbered and nodded in agreement.

"Where are they? Do they live or is it they who roast on the fire?" demanded Walks Alone, digging his fingers into the stringy muscles at the base of the woman's neck.

Biting back her pain, the old woman writhed beneath his grasp and pointed to the river as tears poured down her wrinkled face.

"Do not think that I am a fool," said Walks Alone, pinching even harder, causing the woman to scream in spite of his counsel. "No one could swim in that water. They would die."

"Not swim. They took a floater," screeched the old woman as she struggled to free herself.

Walks Alone quickly extracted the information about the floater from the old woman, learning all that he could about the use of it and what little else she was able to tell him about their quarry.

Then, before Broken Tooth realized what was to happen, Walks Alone tilted the woman's head back, forcing the chin up to an impossible angle, and then further, stilling all protest, the trachea jutting out at an unnatural angle. Then there was a sharp snap, and Walks Alone dropped the woman to the ground like a handful of offal, and walked away.

Broken Tooth stood motionless, his bloodstained hands empty and stared down at the woman's broken body. Somehow this death bothered him more than the unspecific carnage that had gone before. A small child crept to the woman's side and began to weep, ignoring his presence and the possibility of death.

Broken Tooth turned his back on the pair and walked away, leaving the child to his grief, the fact registering dully on his mind. The act made him uncomfortable. He had never thought of Toads grieving, preferring to think of their differences. Grieving made them seem too human. He did not wish to think that they shared common emotions.

Broken Tooth joined Walks Alone in examining the floater, the only one that was still intact. The sight of it made him uneasy, and the sight of the swollen river made him even more uncomfortable. Broken Tooth cleared his throat several times before he spoke.

"Why do you look at this thing so hard, my brother?" he asked courteously, careful not to offend his companion. "Surely you do not plan to follow Emri and the Toad out onto the river! Such a thing would result in our death. Emri and the Toad must be dead by now, sucked beneath these cold waters and devoured by the Water God. Let us make our way back to the tribe and tell what we have learned. It is enough. The totem has been avenged."

"You do not know that. You merely wish it with your cowardly spirit," replied Walks Alone, uncaring whether he gave offense or not. "Emri is clever and the Toad is unlike his clan, showing courage and perseverance. This is a Toad thing. Emri is with a Toad. They escaped in one of these floaters and may still be alive. If they still live, I shall find them and kill them. If they are dead, I will look on their bodies and know it to be true. Then, and only then, will the totem be avenged."

He turned and made as if to push the floater off the rocky ledge and into the river. Stunned by the words, Broken Tooth watched him, his eyes filled with dismay.

"Go back to the tribe and tell them what we have seen or overcome your Toad-like spirit and follow where the river leads, it is all the same to me," said Walks Alone as he glanced at Broken Tooth, his face cold with disdain.

The man's harsh words jolted Broken Tooth from his lethargy. And much as he wanted to return to the tribe, he was determined not to be bested by Walks Alone. His eyes hardened and his jaw firmed, and he picked up his end of the floater and dragged it to the water's edge.

He had one last glimpse of the Toad camp as the river seized them and flung them past the rock-strewn camp. Smoke and mist concealed much, and for that he was thankful. Soon only his mind's eye retained the image of the few remaining survivors, all under ten summers, none of whom would survive the turning of the year.

His heart hung heavy in his breast as they hurtled down the dark, mist-shrouded river, as much for what lay behind as for what lay ahead.

CHAPTER THIRTEEN

"**I**'m hungry," quavered a thin voice.

Emri stirred beneath the fur, fighting his way back from the bonds of deep sleep.

"Where are we? What is this place? Who is this woman, and why does my head hurt?" complained the voice.

Emri's eyes snapped open and he turned his head in the direction of the speaker. Hawk! Against all expectations, Hawk was sitting upright, holding his head with one hand and fending off the rough ministrations of Mosca.

"Oh, my friend, I did not expect to see you again, this side of the land of our ancestors," cried Emri as he scrambled to his knees and gripped Hawk's shoulder tightly.

"I may join them yet if I do not eat soon," muttered Hawk. "My head pounds as though someone is using it for a drum and my belly is as empty as a starved calf. Where are we? Who is this person and where is the river?" he added with a groan, rubbing his eyes gingerly.

"Oh, Hawk, there is too much to tell to answer all your questions quickly," Emri replied shakily. "Lie back and rest. I will find food. When your belly is full, we will speak." Easing Hawk back into a comfortable position, Emri tucked the blanket around Hawk's thin body and then picked up his spear and club and began to push aside the branches that covered the opening.

"Wait! I promise I shall die if you do not tell me where we are and who this person is and—"

"Oh, Hawk, even on the edge of death you do not change," Emri said with a laugh, joy filling him like an overflowing vessel.

"We are far from the Toads, having escaped by way of the river in a floater. This person is Dawn, my woman, and that is all for now," he said, holding up a hand and forestalling the tumult of new questions that he knew would be gathering on Hawk's lips. "I must find food or we will all be joining our ancestors!"

Exiting the branch shelter, followed by Mosca, who gamboled and pounced at his heels, Emri strode into the dense underbrush, all but overwhelmed with happiness, for he had truly expected Hawk to die.

Fortunately, Mosca's energetic forays flushed a fat rabbit from beneath a bush, and the young cat bounded after it and killed it with a snap of his powerful jaws. Emri seized the rabbit before Mosca could carry it off into the brush, tucking it into the front of his tunic, ignoring the cat's squalls of displeasure.

Only after they had flushed and killed two more rabbits and a large red tuft-eared squirrel did Emri allow the cat to keep the next creature, a slow-moving animal who stood up on its hind legs and blinked sleepy eyes at them, its small paws folded across its chest. The animal was unknown to Emri and it was doubtful that he could have taken it from the cat, for Mosca was snarling and hissing in a serious manner, clutching his prey with fully extended claws.

Emri left the cat to make his meal, and gathered a large pile of fat black berries that grew in profusion on low, thorny runners at the edge of the stream. He also gathered a handful of the green leaves that grew nearly in the water itself and possessed a sharp, biting flavor that he had learned to like under Hawk's tutelage. Filling his pouch with berries and leaves, he returned to camp, thankful that he had found food so easily, as all of them—not only Hawk—were badly in need of full bellies.

Entering the shelter, he was greeted by the sight of Hawk and Dawn chattering together as though they had known each other all their lives.

"Emri! Hawk does not remember anything at all about the fight!" Dawn exclaimed as Emri placed the rabbits down in front of the fire. "He cannot remember any of what happened!"

"Nothing?" asked Emri, staring at his friend in amazement.

"Nothing," confirmed Hawk. "The last thing I remember, we were sitting by the river planning how we might take a floater out of the Toad's camp as spirits. After that there is nothing in my mind but this terrible pain and the pounding of drums."

And it seemed to be so, for even though they questioned him most closely and filled him in on the details of their journey, it remained a lost time for Hawk, and one that was never regained.

Having no other explanation, they eventually concluded that Hawk's spirit had roamed with the ancestors during the time that he had lain as though dead, and that for some unknown reason, his spirit had chosen to return. Emri and Dawn treated him with great respect and awe for several days until his boisterous good humor, which seldom treated things seriously, caused them to act in a more normal fashion.

Still, it was a long time before the headaches and dizziness left him, and his vision was often plagued by double images and blurring, a fact that he did his best to conceal from his friends. The wound on his head healed, but the hair that grew above the spot turned white, taking on the appearance of a broad, outstretched wing, giving further credence to his name.

They spent several days and nights in the shelter by the stream as Hawk regained his strength, deciding where to go and what to do.

Hawk was pleased with the spot where they were camped and saw no reason to go any further.

"We are safe here, no one will find us," he argued. "There is good water and the hunting is easy; animals nearly fall over each other, offering themselves up to our spears. What need is there to travel further? I say that we stay."

Dawn was divided, seeing the wisdom in Hawk's

argument, but she thought further ahead than the immediacy of filling her belly and saw other problems. "But what of others?" she asked. "It is not good to remain alone. We three are enough for now, but it is better to be part of a tribe."

"We have done well enough without one up until now," said Hawk. "We three are our own tribe."

"What if both of you are hurt by some large animal?" asked Dawn. "And what about a mate for Hawk? And then there is the birthing. It is always best to have a healer at such times. And what about the Cold Time, when animals will not offer themselves to our spears and hunger will grow in our bellies; then it is best to number more than three."

"We are great hunters," protested Hawk. "With two such as we, your belly will never be empty!" But it was a feeble boast and he did not deny the wisdom of her other comments.

Emri remained silent, merely nodding his head as Dawn spoke. Under her skillful questioning, she drew out his thoughts.

"This is a good place, he agreed, looking about him at the pleasant clearing that they had all come to enjoy, "but Dawn is right in that it would be best to join another tribe. There would be safety against enemies and the Cold Time."

"There is something more than safety in your thoughts," said Hawk, studying his friend through narrowed eyes. "You are not afraid of enemies or of Cold Time. We are brothers to the lion and have much courage; there is some other reason in your heart."

Emri smiled at Dawn and Hawk, who sat cross-legged in the glow of the fire, watching him with knowledgeable eyes. "Ah, you know me too well, my friends," he said with a laugh. "It is true that there is another reason." He looked down at the cat curled at his side and rubbed its tufted ears.

"I wish to know what lies ahead," he said quietly. "I wish to see the Cold Lands and the great mountains of ice with my own eyes and know what people and animals might live there. The thought of it fills my dreams when

I sleep and even when I wake. It has a hold on my heart that will not loosen till I am there."

"All the way to the Cold Lands?" Dawn said fearfully, wrapping her arms around her as though she felt the chill already. "But, Emri, there are no animals or people in the Cold Lands. It is not possible to live there."

"The old stories say that our people lived there once. My father told me so and I have always dreamed of seeing it myself. Never did I think to do so. To come so close and not go . . ." Emri's voice faltered and trailed away but the others did not speak. "But I would see for myself," he said firmly. "And if you are right, perhaps we will find better hunting grounds and other tribes along the way whom we might choose to join."

They argued the issue back and forth for several days and nights, and in the end, the sheer enormity of the idea won Hawk over and he became as strong a proponent as Emri.

Dawn was persuaded less easily and her dark features were stern and unsmiling as Emri and Hawk sought to persuade her. In the end, still fearful and unconvinced, she agreed to the plan reluctantly, because it was clear to her that Emri would not be dissuaded.

She thought with fear of all she had heard of the Cold Lands, a place of unrelenting cold where the snow and ice lay upon the land as high as mountains, and never melted, not even in the heat of Warm Time.

Fear curled around Dawn's heart with fingers of ice. Visions of death began to creep into her mind while she slept, visions of being buried beneath heavy, smothering layers of blue-whiteness. And strangely, the visions were silent, there was no sound at all, not even when she opened her mouth and screamed. Nor was there anyone in the dreams to hear her.

Frightened though she was, she said nothing, but took even greater precautions than usual, making certain that they were well supplied and that they took no unnecessary chances that might bring them to harm. In this, she was well-humored, for Emri and Hawk respected her sense of caution, knowing that it was in their own best interests.

"We can take no more food with us, Little Mother," Hawk said one bright morning. "The floater is loaded more heavily than is normal. To carry more would be dangerous. I am certain that we will find food along the way. The groundfoods grow well and the animals are plentiful, thanks be to the Gods."

"It is always wise to carry food with you when you travel," replied Dawn, drawing a certain amount of reassurance from an adequate amount of supplies.

"But, Little Mother," Hawk replied with a smile, "there are no more squirrels or rabbits within a day's walk, for they are all lying smoked in our pouches. And the woods will be silent after we are gone, for we have also taken all of the birds and everything else that dared to walk, crawl, or fly past our camp. Even the berries are stripped from the bushes and the last fish speared from the stream. If we continue to gather, there will be no room left for us in the floater!"

Dawn was forced to smile, for even though Hawk exaggerated, there was more than a little truth to his words and even she had to admit that they were more than adequately provisioned.

Still, it was a bitter moment when last she looked on the camp that had sheltered them so happily, and she turned her steps to the water with a heavy heart.

The days passed one upon the other, each much the same as the day before, and they fell into a routine that satisfied most, if not all, of their needs.

Nights were spent upon the land, the floater always beached while it was still light, so that they might land safely and set up camp before dark.

They took to the water shortly after daybreak each morning in order to make as much distance as possible.

They found that it was possible for three people to sit upright in the floater at the same time, but only because none of them were large. Even so, it was a tight fit and scarcely comfortable, causing leg cramps and backaches before the sun reached its zenith.

The additional weight of their provisions were an

unexpected bonus, providing the tricky craft with a greater stability and ease of handling that they welcomed.

The only real problem was Mosca, who hated the craft and the water more and more with every passing day. At first Emri had hoped that the cat would lie quietly if given a piece of meat or a bone, but such did not prove to be the case, and it was necessary to catch the cat and place him inside a leather pouch at the start of every day. Soon, they all wore a variety of long angry scratches and felt the coldness of the cub's displeasure when he was released at night. Emri feared that Mosca would disappear one night and not return, but so far that had not happened.

The differences in the land and the foliage grew more pronounced as they traveled steadily north. Some of the trees were new to them, taller and wider than those they were familiar with. The bark was dark red in color and shaggy in texture. The lowest branches were far above their heads, and the ground was thick and spongy with their cast-off needles. Pines of lesser dimensions, as well as fragrant cedar and a wide variety of oaks, were also to be found.

The Endless Waters provided a constantly changing scene. Biters remained all too plentiful, but other than circling the floater and occasionally bumping it, they caused no harm. More welcome were the water beasts, whose sleek heads and bright dark eyes examined them with quick glances before diving beneath the waves.

Most welcome of all were the creatures they came to call water-men; long, graceful, and silky pelted, with long tails and intelligent bewhiskered humanlike faces, they often swam right up to the floater and peered at them curiously. The strange water-men were often seen floating on their backs, far from land, wrapped in the long thick streamers of water-weed. They were seemingly unconcerned by any of the dangers around them, although the travelers had once seen one taken by a biter, and many of the water-men wore circular biter scars on their sleek pelts.

Most awesome of all were the large gray fish, larger

than ten dwellings heaped together, who swam in large groupings in the direction from which they themselves had come. Although they were frightening by their very size, the huge fish took no notice of them at all, and after a time, the humans came to appreciate the sight of them without the pang of accompanying fear.

They learned the rhythms of the water, learned to read the waves and perceive the patterns of the currents. Most important, they learned the signs of the weather and were careful to head for land at the slightest sign of a storm, for their craft was delicate at best and they had no wish to capsize in the cold, rough waters. And always they were careful to remain as close to the land as possible, yet avoiding the choppy waves that developed close to shore.

All things considered, they were happy with themselves and with their progress. It seemed, for once, that nothing would go wrong.

CHAPTER FOURTEEN

Broken Tooth and Walks Alone had been more fortunate than Emri and Dawn, for they suffered few of the dangers that the larger craft had encountered. Their floater was nearly a third smaller than Emri's and was weighted down with a variety of fishing gear, poles, spears, nets, and clubs, as well as numerous other items that the Toads had been too lazy to remove from previous trips. These served as ballast, and the weight of the two full-grown men stabilized the craft to such a degree that it compensated for many of their mistakes, allowing them to remain upright instead of spilling them into the racing waters.

It was all a matter of balance, which Broken Tooth and Walks Alone were quick to realize. Unable to speak to each other due to the incredible speed and roar of the river, it was soon obvious that they would be forced to trust their reflexes and their instincts, and pray to the Gods that they were right.

Frightened at first, Broken Tooth soon found the speed exciting and whooped aloud as he dug his stick into the surging waters. The craft seemed to respond to his excitement, leaping rocks and dodging obstacles deftly, as though it were alive.

Walks Alone had no liking for the speed, the water, or the craft. His stomach felt queasy and he blinked rapidly to hold back a sense of dizziness. He would have given anything, even his heavy black bear robe with claws as long as his hand, to be back on land, but he was determined not to show any sign of weakness in front of Broken Tooth. And so they continued.

They had no opportunity to be afraid when they reached the mouth of the river, for a monstrous wave thundered in from the ocean and, catching them in its grip at the end of its surge, dragged them back with it, and they passed through the dangerous rocks on a crest of white water.

They were carried far out onto the Endless Waters and then seized by the current. They found themselves helpless against the powerful flow that forced them in a direction opposite to that in which they wished to go. The current tugged them relentlessly south and the waves hammered at them, flinging them time and again onto the rocky shore.

Finally, unable to claw their way free, they allowed the waves to carry them toward shore, onto a small smooth beach littered with seaweed and silvery smooth tree limbs, surrounded on three sides by steep, unclimbable cliffs.

They rested that night in the shelter of the cliffs, which did nothing to protect them from the cold wind that blew in from the water. Their fire, built of the smooth, salt-impregnated wood, crackled and burned fiercely, sparking and snapping with colors—greens, blues, pinks, and purples—that they had never seen before. But the beauty of the fire did little to comfort them, for they were cold and their bellies were empty and they were far from home in a place they neither knew nor understood.

Walks Alone left the fire and walked down to the water's edge, his toes buried in the cold foaming froth. He looked up at the dark sky, bright with the glow of the ancestors' fires, and hugged himself against the cold, cutting wind. He found the star that his eyes always sought out, believing that its fire was the one that warmed his own ancestors.

Walks Alone was a brave man, capable of enduring much pain, but the loss of his family had never left him. Even in times of pleasure the pain was there, like a dull ache, constant and unforgiving. Walks Alone often walked out on dark nights and found the star, drawing comfort from the knowledge that those who had passed before were with him still.

He remembered his father, Long Club, a strong silent man who had spoken rarely, but who had taught the eager youngster all that he knew, and had never been too busy for his company. In his prime, before he was taken by the terrible wasting disease that had turned him into little more than bone, he had once killed a bison with a single blow to the head from his massive club.

Walks Alone pictured his father sitting in front of the fire with his older brother, Sharp Spear, who had died shortly after his passage to manhood, ripped apart by a great black bear whom he had disturbed while cutting stone for spearpoints in a cave. That same bear whom Walks Alone had tracked down alone and killed with spear and knife, the same bear whose pelt lay waiting for him beside his own campfire.

Walks Alone lifted his hands, palms outstretched, and spoke to the stars. "Aid me in my search, Father. Lend me your courage to face the dangers that will come. Lend me your wisdom to follow where there is no trail. And lend me your strength to avenge the totem."

The stars glittered brightly and the wind changed direction, plucking at Walks Alone's hair and singing an eerie tune as it strummed against the face of the cliffs. Walks Alone lowered his hands to his sides, no longer cold, and felt that his prayers had been heard.

CHAPTER FIFTEEN

There was a delicate balance needed in navigating the floater. Although it was necessary to put a safe distance between themselves and the shore to avoid the rough water, it was also necessary to avoid going out too far. There was a powerful current that swept through the Endless Waters, flowing in the direction from which they had come. Once, they had inadvertently ventured out too far and had been taken by this current. They had fought furiously to break free of its grasp and were swept a half-days' voyage in the wrong direction before they were able to pull free.

Emri had also noticed a disquieting factor for the past several days: the water was growing increasingly rough. Inshore, the waves were choppy and steep, often pounding against a rocky shoreline that offered no safe landings. Yet the strip of calm water that lay between the offshore turbulence and the deepwater current appeared to be growing more and more slender with every passing day.

Soon, it became obvious even to Hawk and Dawn. The sound of the wind was different, as was the action of the waves. The land itself jutted out in front of them, forcing them to change their direction, paddling west instead of north. The stony cliffs they had become accustomed to dropped lower and lower till they were scarcely more than four man-heights above them, and in some places less. Slowly they realized that they were paralleling a great headland that swung far out into the Endless Waters; and as they approached what must be the tip of its outer edge, the wind and the currents became chaotic and dangerously violent.

To make matters worse, a thick white fog descended on them, enveloping land as well as water and muffling all sound in a curious manner. Fearful of continuing without knowing what lay on the other side of the headland, and even more afraid of becoming lost in the fog, they took advantage of a brief gap in the clinging mist and beached the floater on a narrow stretch of sand.

They wedged the floater above the high-water mark between two small wind-bent trees and crept inland to investigate.

The going was difficult, and only Mosca, delighted as always to be free of the hated leather bag, seemed to enjoy the expedition. The wind blew constantly, spitting sand in their faces and chilling them to the marrow with the thick wet fog that shrouded everything above knee level.

They heard the water on the other side of the slender point of land, but were unable to see it. Reluctant to continue in the dense fog for fear of falling over some unseen precipice, they returned to the beach, where they spent three long days locked in by the fog, attempting to stay warm and dry.

A sturdy shelter was built of storm-tossed tree trunks and limbs that had been deposited in thick layers all along the shore by past storms. These were formed into a low dwelling and then covered with skins and weighted down around the edges with rocks. A central fire did much to keep them warm, but once they left the shelter, the cold damp wind bit through their clothing and left them feeling little better than naked.

Discomforted as they were by the weather, food was not a problem. They had an ample supply of smoked provisions, and Hawk stalked the coast despite the fog and stinging rain, returning to camp with his pouch filled with all manner of strange and peculiar items. The bearded mollusks, which he prized from the rocks at low tide in large numbers, were rubbed clean and then placed in a leather bag with a small amount of salt water

and a larger amount of fresh water, which accumulated in
the rocks above them and cascaded down to the beach.
The bag was then suspended above the fire until the
water bubbled and the shells opened. Hawk then added
other things he had gathered: red, wriggling many-
legged creatures covered with hard skins that reminded
Emri of spiders, pulpy brown tubes that squirmed and
tried to burrow into one's hand, and long strands of
green and brown sea grass. All of these things, and often
others, were added to the steaming pouch. The resulting
brew, Emri thought privately, was more to be valued for
its heat than for its taste or texture.

Dawn had few such misgivings and ate everything,
watching Hawk with interest as he prepared food in a
manner that was entirely foreign to her. She often
accompanied Hawk on his explorations, holding the
sack, and allowing him to step unburdened into the icy
waters in search of his foodstuffs.

Mosca remained with Emri while the others went
on their forays, preferring to stay as far from the water as
possible. The cat had continued to grow, and as Emri
noted with sudden surprise, he could no longer accu-
rately be called a cub.

Nearing the end of his first year, Mosca was taking
on the look of an adult cave lion. His front legs were
already developing the muscular definition that would,
in adult years, enable him to clasp the neck of a young
mastodon, the cave lions' favorite prey, and bite into the
jugular.

Emri noted that Mosca was sprouting a shaggy dark
mane ruff, which would some day line his head and neck.
Already, he had much of his size and was nearly as tall
and as heavy as Emri. As an adult cat, Mosca would be a
third again as long as Emri in length and would weigh
easily two or three times as much as an adult human
male. But for now, he resembled nothing so much as a
small child who tries on his father's cloak and can not fill
it out.

Still, considering Mosca's early days, sucking goat's

milk out of a gourd, Emri felt all the pride of a mother as he observed the strong healthy cat.

The fog and the persistent drizzling rain cleared on the evening of the third day. Emri, Hawk, and Dawn scrambled to the top of the low promontory and eagerly scanned the view that spread before them. What they saw was far from encouraging.

Ahead of them there was nothing but water and more water, swirled and swept by myriads of conflicting currents. Far distant, all but concealed by low-lying clouds, was a dark smudge that might possibly be land.

To the right of them lay the mouth of an immense double-lobed bay, the source of the downpouring of waters, no doubt fed by a large river as indicated by the heavy brown stain that spread upon the dark blue of the Endless Waters.

Straight ahead, slightly inside the arms of the headlands was what appeared to be a small island although it was impossible to make out any details. There seemed to be no easy way to continue their journey, and for the first time since they had begun their voyage, Emri felt his spirits flag.

No one spoke for a time. None was willing to voice the obvious, each knowing without speaking the disappointment that was filling Emri like a bitter herb upon the tongue.

Dawn and Hawk left him there on the promontory, staring out across the Endless Waters as the setting sun smoothed the surface and turned it as gold as flame.

Dawn and Hawk were busy with the fire and the evening meal when Emri finally descended from the heights. They kept themselves occupied with small tasks, unwilling to meet his eye.

"I think I see a way that we might go," said Emri, the words dropping like stones in the pool of silence. Dawn looked up, a gasp of sharp dismay escaping from her lips before she could bite it back. She gazed at Emri and then wrapped her arms around her swollen belly, as though protecting it from harm.

"How can this be?" asked Hawk. "I saw no passage of safety. There is danger on all sides."

"We will head for the island," replied Emri, blind to Dawn's distress, so involved was he in the working of his plan. Crouching on the ground, he smoothed out the sand with the palm of his hand and drew with a small stick.

"Here is where we are now," he said, poking the point of the bulging headland. "Here is the island. And beyond it lies the land. This is my plan. We will leave tomorrow morning and head straight out into the Endless Waters. I believe that the current will push us straight toward the island. Once we are there, we can stay the night and rest, then leave in the morning and take ourselves back to the land on the far side. It cannot be so far. I could see it clearly."

"Could you?" said Dawn. "And could you also see the place where our bodies will lie and be eaten by biters and fish? Tonight, look you up into the sky and find a campfire where our spirits will not rest because no one will have sung them safely to the world of our ancestors.

"And know you that you will kill us with this dream vision. It is not my vision and I do not wish to die. It is cold here, Emri, and wet, and my bones ache and I fear for the life that I carry in me. Let us go back now, while we still live, for I am afraid."

She looked at Emri, her large brown eyes pleading even more eloquently than her words, and tears formed as he looked at her. The tears trickled down her cheeks unchecked and Emri was astounded at the depth of her feeling.

Hawk laid a hand on Dawn's shoulder in a tentative manner. For the first time, as though a cloud had moved away from the sun, Emri saw the love and caring in Hawk's eyes that he had somehow never noticed before.

Emri looked from one to the other and wondered how he had been so unobservant. Dawn's distress was obviously deeply rooted, and Hawk's unguarded gaze left Emri with a sick feeling in the pit of his stomach.

"I did not know you felt so strongly," he said huskily, the words falling from his tongue like stones. "My heart tells me that this is a thing that I must do, but you are a part of my heart as well and I cannot go if you are unwilling."

Dawn had been prepared for arguments and even for stubborn refusals. The one thing she had not expected was acquiescence.

"We will go back," Emri said steadily. "Somewhere we will find a tribe; somewhere where it is less cold and wet. I . . . I did not realize that the two of you felt this way. My dream was too strong to allow me to see into your hearts. I am sorry."

His strength seemed to leave him then, and he crouched down beside the fire and began to feed it sticks that it did not need. Mosca, totally disinterested in human affairs and unhappy with being ignored, butted Emri in the chest as he had often done as a cub, demanding attention. Without thought or feeling, Emri reached up and scratched the cat on its creamy chest and throat.

Dawn began to sob, tears pouring down her face. She sank to her knees and hurled herself into Emri's arms, crying convulsively, her words all but unintelligible. Hawk stood with awkward arms, not knowing what to' do.

"Hush, Dawn, I did not mean to cause you such pain," Emri said softly, cradling Dawn in his arms and smoothing back the damp tendrils that curled away from her temples.

"But do not fear for the child. I am certain that he will be born big and strong and full of brave spirits, for he too is brother to the lion. Nor would I let you come to harm. Somewhere, there will be a place for us. We will find it and all will be well."

Strangely, these words only caused Dawn to cry harder, and she covered her face with her hands so that Emri might not see her loss of courage and despise her.

Hawk sat back, rubbing the cat who refused to be

ignored, observing the two people whom he had come to
care for more than any others alive. And yet, as he
stroked Mosca, feeling the cat rumble contentedly
beneath his hands, he felt as though he were being torn
in two.

Emri was as a brother to him; together they had
slain Mosca's mother and survived an entire Cold Time
on their own in the den of the cave lions. Together they
had killed the saber-toothed tiger, totem of Emri's tribe
and fierce predator who had sought to slay them.

They had saved each other's lives more times than
could be counted on two hands. They had laughed
together and cried together, they had experienced
much. If Emri had a vision, it was Hawk's as well. If
Emri's vision told them to go north, then it was Hawk's
destination as well.

But Dawn was his to consider also. For the two of
them were much alike in many ways. She accepted his
liking for food-gathering and praised his knowledge
often. She learned from him, willingly, discovering new
foods with the same joy and excitement that Emri would
have felt over a beautiful spearpoint. Together they had
explored the tide pools and new foliage of the rapidly
changing forest and discovered that which was edible
and often, with giggles and awful faces, that which was
not. Together they had played with Mosca in the quiet
times and planned the decoration of a garment that
Dawn was fashioning for the child. And they had smiled
at each other often, sharing thoughts that held no
meaning for anyone else.

Dawn had become Hawk's best friend, his play-
mate, his love, even though he did not realize it, and he
felt his heart ache within him as she cried out her
distress.

He felt as though he were being ripped in two. Part
of him felt as though he were dying with the death of
Emri's dream, and raged at the wrongness of it.

Yet the other half of him agreed with Dawn, and
wanted to hold her and take her far away and keep her
safe from the danger and madness of Emri's plan.

And so, agreeing with both of them, and helpless against their mutual pain, he could do nothing but share their grief.

CHAPTER SIXTEEN

Walks Alone and Broken Tooth studied the waves from their small beach much as they would have observed an animal they wished to hunt. They learned the pattern of the tides and the different types of currents. Finally, after being trapped on the small beach for more days than the fingers on one hand, they succeeded in breaking out of the prevailing current, and fought their way back in the direction they thought Emri and Hawk had taken.

They had studied the ways of the water well and were soon making excellent progress, although Walks Alone still agonized that they might have lost their quarry. He drove Broken Tooth and himself with a single-minded determination, rising early while the mist was still on the water and landing late, often making a rude camp in the moonlight and sleeping with empty bellies.

Their efforts were rewarded late one afternoon by the sight of a single tendril of smoke that rose high in the air, some distance ahead of them.

Broken Tooth shouted aloud and pointed out the white plume to Walks Alone, whose eyes were bright with anticipation. In truth, even he had begun to wonder if Emri and the Toad were still alive.

Through the remainder of that day, they drove the floater through the water until their muscles ached and burned with the agony of the tedious repetitious action and the darkness closed around them like a fist. Walks Alone would have continued on, despite the darkness and the discomfort, but Broken Tooth spoke out, protesting.

"Forget the pain that is in my arms and legs, my brother," said Broken Tooth, who doubted that his companion had ever considered it, "but if we continue on in the dark, it would be all too easy to strike a rock or a log and destroy the floater." He paused. "And ourselves," he muttered beneath his breath.

"It would be wise to stop now, while we are still able to see the shore. We cannot be far from them. Having found them once, we will find them again."

Walks Alone slumped against the high retaining edge of the floater and mulled over Broken Tooth's words, feeling the cold of the water beneath the floater, and the twitch of exhausted muscles. He knew that Broken Tooth was right, but he hated to stop. He felt as though he were making progress as long as he was moving. When he stopped, frustration gnawed at him like a rodent among the roots. But fear of the water, which became more intense in the dark, and the fact that the smoke could no longer be seen, finally convinced him. Wordlessly, he headed the floater in toward shore.

They made a rough camp and chewed on tough, tasteless strips of dried meat. Unable to rest, exhausted though he was, Walks Alone took his bearings, then set off through the forest, thinking that perhaps he might be able to find the enemy camp more easily at night, guided by the sight and smell of their fire.

But in this he was foiled, for the wind was blowing inland, sweeping all possible scent away from him, and there was no sight of another fire. In the end, hearing the baying of dire wolves in the distance and afraid of becoming lost in the unfamiliar forest, he was forced to turn back.

They began again next morning, scarcely stopping for a fist full of berries and raw fish before taking to the floater once more.

They were alert now knowing that the quarry was near. As they paddled, their eyes scanned the gray waters. Then, Broken Tooth's sharp eyes caught sight of the deep wedge cut in the damp sand of the spit and the dark line that trailed away into the water.

They beached their floater in the same spot, fitting their craft in the wedge, and made their way into the forest, following the trail of footprints as though tracking an animal to its lair.

Walks Alone's hands tightened around his club and his heartbeat quickened. The floater was gone, but perhaps one or more of the trio had remained behind. If so, they had breathed their last.

But the camp was empty and none of their possessions remained. Walks Alone, thwarted at every turn, stared about him, reading the signs of a long encampment. It was obvious, from the neatly constructed shelter to the depth of the ash and the mounds of shells at the edge of the clearing, that the enemy had stayed here for some time.

While he had been trapped on the cold desolate beach, they had been here, eating, drinking, and warming themselves by the fire. They had laughed and talked while he endured the freezing rain and battled the cold currents.

A scream of rage rose in his throat, and swinging his club high above his head, he assaulted the shelter. He slammed his club into it repeatedly until he stood among the splintered ruins, sweat pouring down his face, his chest heaving with exertion.

They set out immediately, Broken Tooth eyeing Walks Alone nervously and wondering if perhaps the man had gone mad. They heaved the floater back into the water and once more began to follow the invisible trail.

Through the days that followed, they occasionally caught sight of smoke plumes rising in the air, and found the campfires, still warm and smoking in the cold, damp air, but never did they catch sight of their quarry. They slept little and ate less, and Walks Alone took on the look of one who was obsessed. His eyes glittered like bits of mica and his cheeks became hollow and gaunt. His hair grew matted and held bits of leaves and tiny twigs from the rare moments he could be persuaded to rest. Broken

Tooth watched him carefully in case the man lost all reason and attempted to vent his rage on him.

They spotted the telltale plume of smoke again, early one morning when the sun shone down warmly and the wind blew gently out of the west, causing Broken Tooth to wish that he were at home on familiar ground, instead of trapped in the floater with a mad man. He dreaded the landing, dreaded the rage that he knew would follow as they explored yet another empty campsite.

Yet this morning was to be different, for it was apparent upon landing even to his less skilled reading, that the camp had only recently been abandoned. His senses quickened and he swung about, alert, seeking other signs that might lead him to his quarry. The quicker it was over, the sooner he might return to the tribe and the woman and family he missed so badly.

Walks Alone was already out of the driftwood dwelling, running up the steep slope toward the highest point of land. Broken Tooth followed on his heels.

"There! See you, there!" Walks Alone hissed exultantly, his arm all but quivering with tension. Broken Tooth sighted along the pointing arm and there, so small as to appear but a dark spot on the crest of a wave, he saw the flash of silver as a stick lifted clear of the water.

"We have them now," muttered Walks Alone, his eyes still fastened on the elusive prey, "we have them now."

But Broken Tooth, watching the floater grow more distant with every passing heartbeat, outlined against a rapidly darkening sky, its passengers no more than a half-formed blur. Broken Tooth felt no exultation, no joy, only fear that the chase, like some endlessly recurring nightmare, would never be done.

CHAPTER SEVENTEEN

After the fire was banked for the night, Hawk, Emri, and Dawn lay down and covered themselves with their furskins, Hawk on one side of the fire and Emri and Dawn on the other with Mosca at their feet.

It was over. It was done. The decision had been made to turn back, to find another tribe and make their life with them.

Only it was not done. Even though Emri's arms were wrapped around her and he held her no less closely, it seemed to Dawn that she could feel a difference in his body, a slight pulling away of the spirit if not the flesh.

His breath came slow and steady against her hair, but somehow she knew that his eyes were open, staring into the darkness, seeing a vision that still shone bright in his mind.

They lay like that throughout the long night, and even after Emri's body relaxed in sleep, Dawn remained awake turning the problem over and over.

She had won her way, it was true, but would it not work against her in the end? Would Emri always remember that she had caused him to give up his dream? Would she see it in his eyes every time he looked at her, and would he stop caring for her because of it?

As the thin cold rays of light tentively felt their way into the dwelling, Dawn came to a decision. She would go wherever Emri's vision took them. She had followed him through such paths of danger already that there was little reason to stop now. She had given him her love and her trust; if she believed in him, she must do so completely.

A great calm descended over her at the moment of her decision and she knew that she had made the right choice. Slipping from Emri's embrace, she began to pack their belongings.

Emri and Hawk wakened a short time later to the sharp fragrance of willow leaves and spruce tips simmering in a sack of water. This bitter but potent brew would quench their thirst and stimulate flagging muscles during the long day's journey.

On a long green stick she had skewered fresh fish, which were now sizzling above the fire, and she had made flat cakes of berries, sour fruit, and acorn meal mixed with goose fat. The cakes were baking atop hot flat stones carefully placed among the hot coals. Once done, they would travel well and provide sustenance during the long trip, a welcome break from the tough dried meats and smoked fish that was their normal fare.

"Let us eat and leave this place," Dawn said brightly with a smile on her face. "I would see us on the island before dark."

Emri and Hawk stopped what they were doing and looked at her intently, as though they had misunderstood her words.

"I was wrong to speak as I did," she said quietly, though her face burned red with their sudden scrutiny. "I wish to continue on and I will trouble you no more with my worries. There are no problems that we cannot solve, for you are both strong and brave as well as brothers to the lion."

"You must include yourself in that description," Emri said quietly as he gathered Dawn in his arms and hugged her gently, "for never has a woman had such courage as you. Thank you, Little Mother. My heart is full of joy. Know you that I will never let you come to harm; the biters will never gnaw our bones."

Hawk stood to one side and watched the exchange, his heart lurching sideways in his chest and then beating raggedly, thumping so loudly that he was afraid it would be heard. He was glad that the silent trauma had ended, for he had felt the torment of Dawn and Emri as deeply as though it had been his own. And he had been equally disturbed by the discovery of the depth of his feelings for his friend's woman.

But he had been pleased that she was to be spared the rigors of the dangerous journey that Emri had proposed. Even he, with his broader knowledge of floaters and water travel, had been more than a little concerned over the trip to the island. The waters between the mainland and the island were a battleground of conflicting currents. Hawk doubted that they would survive the trip without some serious mishap. Brave though he was, he shivered at the thought of the dangerous voyage.

He opened his mouth to speak and then held his tongue. If the two were agreed, his words would merely cause dissension. Emri was stubborn, and while Dawn had been able to dissuade him, Hawk was unsure that he could or should. If Emri was determined to go, then it was Hawk's responsibility to help him achieve his goal. He could do no less.

They broke camp quickly, loaded their supplies and the bitterly protesting Mosca into the floater, and set forth for the island.

It was a difficult voyage from the first. Neither Hawk nor Emri had expected the currents to be so powerful, and the waves, which they had viewed from the promontory, had seemed much smaller than they actually were.

Despite these problems, they made good progress and were halfway to the island—which now appeared to be no more than an immense heap of rock—when the first clouds appeared on the western horizon.

They were ominous from the very beginning, and perhaps more so because they were so very, very black and threatening, while the sun still danced on the waters around them, like a butterfly on a flower.

Emri and Hawk watched the clouds build, billowing and towering in the sky as though some giant lay just below the horizon blowing the clouds like bubbles upon the water. After one glance, Dawn kept her head down and paddled harder, as though by ignoring it she could deny that it was happening.

When it seemed that the clouds could climb no higher, they began crowding out the blue until the entire sky became dark.

The advance of the clouds had been silent until that moment. Indeed, the wind, which had been gentle and from the north, now dropped completely, leaving them with only the sibilance of the waves and the cries of the birds now winging rapidly shoreward.

Then, in the space of a single heartbeat, everything changed at once. The clouds still boiled overhead, but now they were accompanied by sound, the rush and whistle of the wind, which almost seemed visible so loud and strong was its force, the rumble of thunder and the crack of lightning as yet unseen.

A giant wave picked them up and held them on high for a brief moment, long enough to see the island, their goal, still distant but nearer than it had been, and definitely closer than the mainland. Even if they had not wished it, the current was carrying them north, toward the island as well as directly into the face of the storm. There would be no turning back.

On the crest of the wave, Hawk had turned back to gauge how far they had come and had seen two men standing on the promontory, clearly outlined against the bright sky. One was pointing directly toward them. Startled, he turned and looked at Emri, who had also seen the men and was staring at them as though thunderstruck. Emri turned and met Hawk's gaze, and Hawk saw fear and anxiety there, mirroring his own.

Who were the men? An instant answer sprang to his lips to remain unspoken. Mandris, the shaman of Emri's tribe, had sent the two to kill them, in retaliation for killing the tiger totem. They had watched in fear but, having seen no sign of pursuit, it had seemed that they might have successfully escaped the shaman's reach.

Both heads turned to look at Dawn, but she was still bent to her paddling, looking only forward and down, and had not seen the followers. Another swift glance showed them nothing but empty land behind them, and for an instant they shared the single hope that they had been mistaken.

But the hope faded quickly, realizing that it was but wishful thinking. They had been followed. Now, all they could hope was that they could not be followed to the island, should they be lucky enough to make it.

Perhaps the followers did not have a floater, and even if they did, surely their search for vengeance would not take them out into the dangerous, storm-tossed waters. But no matter what their thoughts, there were no answers to be had. They could but watch and hope.

Even that was to be put off for the time being, for the storm was growing quickly. The wind rose, changing direction and coming at them from the west. It felt as though they had been driven onto the shore, so solid a force was the wind. It was impossible to gain even the smallest advantage and they felt themselves being blown back the way they had come.

They dug their sticks into the water, clawing their way into the wind, pulling with all their strength, but it was no use; the wind was far stronger than they were.

The sky and even the air around them was nearly as black as night. The water leapt and jumped beneath them as though it wished to become part of the sky. It became extremely difficult to keep the craft on an even keel, for the violence of the wind and the water hurled it this way and that as though it were but a bit of foam.

Screaming orders at each other, they fought to remain upright, knowing that to tip for just one instant would be the death of them, the craft would fill with water and they would sink like a stone to the bottom.

Mosca added his voice to that of the others, his frightened wails rising and falling and grating along the edges of the nerves. But no time could be spared for comforting the cat. He would have to take his chances with the rest of them.

Now came the rain. It began without any warning, no sprinkles, no showers, just an instant deluge as though that same giant who had blown the clouds were now pouring bowls of water from the sky above. It cascaded down their bodies, chilling them. Even worse, it trickled into the floater itself.

There was no room to bail it out, even if there had been an extra pair of hands to do so. But Dawn, sensing the danger immediately, pulled loose the furskin she was crouching on, which had shielded her from contact with the cold skin of the floater, and tucked it in between their bodies and the rim as best she was able, thus causing the water to trickle over the edge, rather than enter the craft.

It was impossible to see now and Emri had lost all sense of direction. He could not even tell which way they were moving, or if they were even moving at all. For all he knew, they were remaining in the same spot, paddling desperately, getting nowhere.

And then, just as they thought that it could get no worse, that the water could rise no higher, that the wind could scream no louder, and the rain could fall no harder, it did. The storm intensified its efforts, seemingly intent on ripping their fragile craft to bits and feeding them to the biters.

Emri prayed to his ancestors and felt a great heaviness in his spirit, in knowing that Dawn's fears had been well-founded and that if they had followed her wishes, they would now be taking shelter on solid land and thanking the Gods that they had not ventured out onto the water.

Then, even those thoughts were dashed from him as a great wave picked them up and literally threw them through the dark air into the crest of another gigantic wave.

That was the start of it. For the remainder of that long morning, they were hurled this way and that by the wind and the waves. They fought with all their strength to remain afloat, driving their sticks deep into the turbulent waters, throwing their weight first one direction then another to center the balance and keep the craft upright.

Water began to collect in the bottom of the floater, and Emri realized that despite the furskin, moisture was seeping through, gathering about their legs. Soon, it was

impossible to ignore the fact that the floater was
becoming even more sluggish and unresponsive than
usual and was lying lower in the water than was the
norm.

Even more frightening was the deeper growl of
water, the growl that Emri had come to recognize as the
sound water made as it was flung against rock with great
violence and then sucked back upon itself. This type of
water was the most dangerous for the floater, for should
it be seized by such a current, there would be no
breaking loose and they would be killed—drowned or
broken on the rocks—before they could free themselves.

It was clear that Hawk and Dawn appreciated the
danger, even if they could not see it, for their efforts
increased even further. Still, the horrible sound grew
both louder and closer, as though the Gods were
laughing at them and their puny attempts.

And then, all in one startling instant, they felt a
giant wave building beneath them, one of the truly
immense waves that came along but seldom, and they
felt the floater rising higher and higher as the wave
crested and began its long slide forward.

At that exact instant, the rain parted and they
glimpsed clearly a shoreline lying but a short distance
away, trees and earth plainly visible as though mocking
them. And between them and the safety of the land lay a
solid line of vicious rocks, their jagged edges battered by
the waves and dripping with storm-tossed foam. Rocks
that would rip through the fragile skin of the floater,
rocks that would tear the life from their bodies.

Dawn screamed as the wave began its long smooth
glide, and all of them bent to their sticks, digging deep
and pulling back as though by the sheer force of their
desperation they could prevent the inevitable.

Faster and faster they went, as the crest of the wave
curled and dropped out from beneath them, succumbing
to its own predestined fate, and then they were weightless, hanging in midair above the streaming rocks.

Impossible though it seemed, Emri took note of
each and every occurrence as it happened, seemingly

strung out in separate silent incidents. First they were hung in midair above the rocks. This, in Emri's mind, was isolated in a kind of golden air, silent, though filled with slow, patient movement.

Then they were falling, again slowly and again in silence. The water appeared far distant and it seemed as though they would hang forever weightless between the sky and the water.

Then sound and movement returned with a rush, and, with it, the loss of hope as the floater struck the water, turned on its side, and spilled them out into the icy, turbulent waters.

CHAPTER EIGHTEEN

The shock of the icy water more than anything else, caused Emri to lash out. In doing so, his hand struck something smooth and hard. His fingers wrapped around the object and clung to it with a life of their own, preventing him from being swept away as the great wave returned to the Endless Waters from which it had come.

Emri felt the sharp grittiness of sand and rock beneath his body as the water sucked him down and back, trying to drag him with it. He dug his feet into the cold thick sludge and fought his way forward, fighting the pull of the receding wave.

He had no time to look for any of the others, despite the fact that his mind was crazed with fear for them, for if he did not save himself from the waters, they would claim him and pound him to death on the rocks.

The sands gave him no solid footing, merely giving way beneath his scrambling toes and his weight. The water was pulling hard against his single hold. He screamed aloud with the fury of his frustration, fearing that he would lose his grip and be swept away, when the waters reached the end of their ebb and then came flooding back, flinging him forward with a great rush.

His fingers were wrenched from the tree root as he hurtled over the rocks where it had wedged and was flung headlong into a tangle of great boulders. His head was ringing and blood was pouring down into his eyes from a gash on his scalp, but he was able to stagger to his feet and hold onto a boulder as the wave that had brought him seethed back into the maelstrom.

"Hawk! Dawn! Mosca!" he screamed into the storm. And from somewhere beyond his limited field of vision, he heard an answering cry, although from who or what he could not discern.

Holding fast to the rocks, he pulled himself from one boulder to the next in the direction of the cry.

The world seemed to be made of water. Despite climbing the rocks, the water was often above his knees, beseiging him in powerful surges. One after the other the waves sucked and pulled at him, as though unwilling to surrender to the land.

The air was filled with water as well. Rain lashed down on him with the force of blows and foam-flecked spume and salt water were dashed against his body at every step. At times it seemed that he took in more water than air.

He continued to call, his throat hoarse with the effort, but there was no answer. He became almost wild with fear and began to run, which was madness considering the terrain, stopping only after he lost his footing on a weed-slick rock and nearly tumbled back into the turbulent water.

He sank down on a rock, wrapped his arms around his body, and rocked back and forth. "Father, do not let me lose them," he whispered. "Send your spirit to help me find them."

Spirits or luck guided his footsteps, for he found his companions on the other side of a massive boulder at the foot of a spill of rocks that had tumbled from the cliff above.

Hawk was sitting on a rock, out of reach of the waves, holding Dawn in his arms. Mosca crouched, drenched and terrified, as close to the humans as he could get.

Emri hurried to Hawk's side, his heart soaring within his breast until he noticed that Hawk was staring at Dawn without moving and that her eyes were closed and her arms hung limp and still.

"Dawn!" cried Emri, flinging himself on his knees and pressing his head to her chest. For a moment, the blood beat a loud tattoo inside his head and he could

hear nothing but his own frantic heartbeat, then he
heard a thin, ragged beat and knew that she still lived.

He looked about him wildly, but there was nothing
to see but the rain and wave-lashed coast, a forbidding
stretch of stones and boulders with the forest rising far
above their heads atop steep and unclimbable cliffs.

As Emri looked around him, searching in desperation for a spot of shelter, Dawn gasped and turned on her
side. Emri turned back, the sound echoing happily in his
ears, but all joy fled as he saw her face twist in pain.
Hawk wrapped his arms around her protectively and she
held his arm with her hands and squeezed hard, as little
whimpering noises slipped through her clenched teeth.

"The child is coming," Hawk said, lifting stricken
eyes to Emri. "The pains are coming often. It should not
happen like this, Emri, they will both die."

"They will not die," said Emri, and picking Dawn
up, he held her close to his chest, her head falling limp
against his shoulder. Turning blindly toward the cliff, he
took one step, then another, away from the water.

In spite of his desperation, which drove him on long
after his legs had lost all feeling in the frigid waters, he
was unable to find any way up the face of the cliff.

Shelter was almost as difficult, and the storm grew
stronger still. They were forced to make do with
crawling under a large slab of rock that lay tilted to one
side like a giant lean-to, propped against an immense
black boulder. The waves snarled a short distance away
but were unable to reach them. Rain and wind had no
such problems, though, and their bodies streamed with
water.

They laid Dawn on the cold uneven stones and
arranged her as best they could, gathering bits of wet
water-weed to soften the harsh bed. But it was doubtful
that she was aware of either the rocks or their efforts, for
she was gone from them, locked in a place of private
pain.

The child was born at the very height of the storm,
and as the wind shrieked and screamed around them,
Emri looked down at the tiny bit of bloody flesh and felt
something twist inside him.

Dawn was pale, as though all of her blood had drained out of her with the birthing, and her flesh was cold. Saddened as Emri was at the loss of the child, he was even more frightened for Dawn. He knew all too well that it was after birthings, even those done with benefit of shelter and warmth with healers and other women to help, that women most often died. It was imperative that they find shelter and build a fire if they were to prevent Dawn from following her child to the land of the spirits.

As though content at having done its worst, the storm faded away to little more than blustery squalls. The sun returned, still masked by towering white clouds, washed clean by the storm, and hung above the waves as though undecided whether to shine or not. It settled for a pale, wintery glow that shed no warmth.

Emri left Hawk with Dawn while he and Mosca set off along the debris-strewn coast to find a place where they might gain access to the forest above.

The going was difficult, rocks and boulders, some four times as large as Emri himself, provided the only footing. Sometimes even that was absent, replaced by stretches of foaming water.

After traveling in an easterly direction for some time and finding no hint of a trail by which they might ascend the cliff, their way was blocked by a fall of rocks. On the other side was nothing but a sheer cliff and storm-whipped water.

Much as he hated to turn back, he was forced to retrace his steps. There was no way to reach the cliffs above. He passed Hawk and Dawn where they lay beneath the rock, Hawk attempting to shield her from the elements with his own small frame. But Emri knew that the cold stone would drain whatever warmth there was in her body. If the birthing and the loss of blood did not kill her, the cold would.

At first it seemed that the new course would be no better. Emri had a brief moment of black despair when he felt that he would find no way up the cliff and they would all die on the wet rocks. His own feet felt like

blocks of ice and it became harder and harder to drive
himself on.

Then, just as he felt that he could go on no longer,
he heard the sound of rushing water, and, rounding a
fallen boulder, found what he had been searching for. It
was a narrow, rock-choked ravine, really little more than
a gully, a cut in the land where water funneled down to
the sea from the land above. Climbing it would be
difficult, but he knew that it could be done.

Emri and Hawk carried Dawn between them, for
the risk was too great that one would fall and take her
with him. Together they climbed the narrow water
course, fighting their way through the icy water, treacherous rocks and broken trees from the forest above, and
just as the weak sun gave up its efforts and slunk below
the waiting horizon, they reached the top of the plateau.

They found themselves in a dense forest of trees
that towered high above their heads. So tall were the
trees, and so massive, that there was little underbrush
and none of the junipers and spruce that Emri had
hoped to find. Broad fat trees with wide-sweeping
branches would provide them with shelter from the
weather.

The ground was spongy underfoot, thick with the
undisturbed accumulation of needles and leaves shed
from the towering giants. The surface of this dense mat
was crosshatched with spaces that allowed moisture to
trickle through. Normally, it would have provided a soft
dry surface, but now it was wet, saturated by the heavy
rainfall and constant drip from the trees above.

As the shadows darkened beneath the tall trees,
Emri knew that they could go no further. His strength
was at an end, and he could tell from Hawk's dragging
steps that he too had reached his limit. As he stood
beneath the dripping canopy, head bowed with exhaustion, he heard Mosca yowling with excitement somewhere just ahead of them.

Emri's head came up, for he knew that only prey
caused this sound in the cat. Signaling Hawk to stay with
Dawn, he left them and hurried forward on shaking legs.

Mosca was easily found by the excited squalls
traveling through the forest for all to hear.

He was but a short distance away, clawing excitedly at the base of a large tree—or what remained of one. At some time in the distant past, the giant had been struck by lightning or had burned in one of the great fires that periodically swept through the forest killing those made susceptible by insects or the rot of age.

The tree had broken off halfway up its great height, the top half toppling to the ground where it had become a nursery for moss and lichen and ferns and a home for insects. Later, after time had rotted the bark and softened the wood beneath it, seeds had settled in its welcoming crevices and saplings had taken root, vying for the small open space its passing had caused in the leafy roof high above.

But it was the lower half of the tree that held Emri's interest, for animals had burrowed between its gnarled roots and made their den beneath its bulk. It was their scent, hanging heavy on the moist air, that had attracted Mosca. But Emri was interested in the shelter, as well as in the food that the creatures would provide.

Emri knelt beside a small half-buried tree trunk and scooped up a handful of round, hard black pellets that lay thick on the mossy ground. Rabbits. So be it. Emri would not have been less determined had the inhabitants of the den been something fierce and dangerous.

Mosca was certainly not going to have much success by his methods. Rabbits did not tend to surface from their burrows when something growled and dug at the entrance. Nor could they be lured out by other means. They would have to be forced out.

Emri called to Hawk and soon he appeared, carrying Dawn in his arms. Emri helped him find a place for her at the base of a large oak whose broad branches had kept the ground beneath it drier than the neighboring pines.

It was beneath this same oak that Hawk and Emri managed to find a dead limb that could be made to suit their needs. Finding dry tinder was more difficult, but knowing that there was the hope of food and warmth gave new energy to their faltering limbs and they

combed the forest looking for bits and pieces dry enough
to burn.

They gathered bird nests and handfuls of leaves and
twigs that were wedged deep in deadfalls, all kept dry by
the dense mat of debris above them. And finally, they
found branches and sticks that were damp but would
burn, given a strong enough blaze.

All of these they brought back to the base of the
tree. A small mound was built at the mouths of four
burrows. All the others, save the main entrance to the
warren, were filled in, packed with moss, dirt, stones,
sticks, and whatever else came to hand.

Mosca was chased off with a larger stick when he
insisted on digging up one of the burrows they had just
filled. He squalled and spat in anger, and hissed
whenever they spoke, assuring him that he would get his
share.

At last they were ready; and Emri bent to the task of
starting the fire. The sticks were not ideally suited for
the purpose, the twirling stick being slightly canted to
one side, but they were dry.

Taking up a bit of stone, Emri dug out a resting
place in the center of the stick that would form the base
for the bottom of the twirling stick.

Once he was satisfied that it would not slip out,
Emri placed the base on the ground and began the
tedious process of twirling the stick between his palms,
starting at the top and rolling it back and forth between
his hands until he reached the bottom of the stick, then,
so quickly that the eye could scarce see any break in the
motion, starting at the top once more.

Over and over he repeated the motion until the
bottom of the rapidly twirling stick began to glow and a
tiny tendril of smoke, almost too small to see, crept out
into the cold, damp air.

Hawk, waiting for that exact moment, fed tiny bits
of dry leaf mold to the glowing spark, and between
them, they nursed it into a healthy blaze.

When the fire was secure, they touched fire to the
piles stacked in front of the burrows and fanned them
with their hands until they blazed.

While not actually wet, the heaps of debris were damp, and the fire created more smoke than real flames, which was exactly what was wanted.

Fanning the smoke with their hands, Emri and Hawk directed it into the open burrows, and after a short time they began to hear high-pitched squeals and whistling squeaks, and sensed as much as heard a kind of panicked rustle from the heart of the warren.

They added new fuel to the piles, taking less care now that the blaze was well begun. The fire bit into the crumbled leaf mold and bits of twigs and the moisture sizzled and steamed and billowed out in a thick acrid white column as well as flowing into the waiting burrows.

Sensing that the moment was at hand, the moment when the terrified rabbits could bear the smoke no longer, their terror of fire greater than their fear of what waited outside, Emri positioned himself in front of the one entrance without a fire. Hawk had no sooner joined him and lifted a stick on high than the first rabbit bolted out of the hole and, dodging both of their blows, ran straight into Mosca, who seized the rabbit in his waiting jaws and broke its neck in one swift motion.

It was but the first of many who sought to escape. Few succeeded. Most ran as fast as their powerful legs would carry them, but some, bulging eyes watering, and dazed by the smoke, staggered out and sat hunched, wheezing painfully until they were dispatched.

When the flow of rabbits ceased, Emri judged that any who remained were dead or dying, and he scraped the burning mounds into one compact fire beneath the oak tree where Dawn lay. His heart gladdened by their success, Emri began adding sticks to the fire, and although they smoked, he was pleased to see that they burned as well.

"Start digging," said Hawk. "I will tend the fire and watch Dawn. I will join you as soon as I can."

Casting one last worried look at Dawn, Emri left her to Hawk's competent hands and directed all of his attention to the problem at hand.

From the great number of rabbits who had emerged
from the ground beneath the tree stump, Emri knew
that it was a large warren. The earth must have been
literally honeycombed with passages, divided only by
thin earthen walls on many levels. Once excavated, it
would provide them with a warm, dry shelter.

Emri and then Hawk, in his turn, attacked the
burrow with fierce determination, shoveling and digging
with branches and bleeding hands. But even with those
efforts, the moon had nearly reached its apex by the time
the burrow was large enough to hold the four of them
comfortably.

Hawk had taken time out from shoveling to skin and
clean the rabbits, giving the entrails and organs to Mosca
but saving the meat and skins. Several carcasses were set
to roast over the fire, but so great was their hunger that
they consumed the meat long before it was fully roasted,
wrenching off strips of the tough gamy meat and
swallowing it nearly whole, scarcely noticing when it
burned their tongues and throats and blistered their lips.

Emri tried to rouse Dawn, to urge her to eat some
of the strength-giving flesh, but though her eyelids
fluttered, she did not waken.

During the course of the excavation, Hawk and
Emri had come upon several nests of baby rabbits, some
still without fur, naked and pink as human infants, dead
in their nests of soft grasses and fur plucked from the
mother's own abdomen. These Hawk carefully placed to
one side, safe from Mosca's voracious appetite.

When the hole was large enough to allow them to sit
upright as well as lie down, they lined the center portion
of the floor with furskins taken from the former inhabitants.

While Emri carried Dawn into the warren and
stripped her wet garments from her chilled body, Hawk
carefully moved the fire to the far end of the hole where
it vented out of the warren through two of the remaining
entrances. Because the area was so small, the fire soon
raised the temperature of the warren to that of a hot
summer day. Soon, even Dawn's flesh had lost its pallor,
and Emri was pleased to note that the unhealthy blue

tinge that had lain just below the surface of her skin was gone as well.

They chafed her hands and spoke to her gently, pleading with her to open her eyes and speak to them, but she did not stir. More disturbingly, the blood still flowed from between her legs, though pink and watery, rather than the dark red that it had been.

Emri felt a coldness, in the center of his being, at the sight of the blood. He looked away, stroking Dawn's brow and calling to her, unwilling to look at the blood, as though by ignoring it he could pretend that it was not happening.

Broken bones, cuts and bites, these he was accustomed to and could face squarely, but birthing problems required special knowledge of a sort that he did not possess. Even seeing Dawn's naked body filled him with a sense of unease, for in his tribe one did not let one's eyes linger on unclothed women past the time of their youth. To do so was considered unclean in some unspoken manner.

"What should we do," Emri asked in a whisper, knowing that Hawk possessed far more healing lore than he.

"I do not know," answered Hawk, his eyes bright with tears. "I do not know what to do but pray to the spirits and beg them not to take her."

"Yes, we will do that," Emri said heavily. "And then we will bury the child and send its spirit on its way. Perhaps the ancestors will be satisfied with its spirit and will spare the mother."

Sitting beside the woman they both loved, Hawk and Emri withdrew into themselves and spoke to the spirits of their ancestors, begging them to spare Dawn and making whatever promises they felt necessary to weight their wishes.

Then, before they gave way to the fatigue that threatened to overtake them, they buried the small body of the child, born long before its time, and said the prayers that would speed its tiny spirit on its way to those who waited to receive it.

Wood was gathered and laid over the entrance to the burrow, where it would be close at hand and would offer some slight protection against roving predators.

Then, lying down beside Dawn and the cat, who was already curled into a tight ball, they gave themselves up to their exhaustion and slept.

CHAPTER NINETEEN

Dawn's eyes were open when Emri wakened, but when he took her in his arms and tried to speak to her, she turned her head away and closed her eyes, tears flowing down her cheeks.

Deeply stricken, knowing that Dawn was blaming him for the loss of the child, Emri held back his words and felt the blackness gather inside him.

The fire was all but extinguished and the cold of the earth was beginning to creep back when Emri rose and left Dawn, who had fallen into a restless sleep. She had turned on her side, drawing her knees up to her chin. Emri was alarmed to see that the flow of blood had not diminished during the night, and now pooled beneath her on the rabbit skins.

Worried, and more than a little frightened, Emri reached over and awakened Hawk. Mosca also wakened, with wide shrill yawns and much stretching of furry limbs, then padded up to the entrance and pushed through the tangle of branches.

"What should we do?" Emri asked in a whisper although it was unlikely that Dawn would hear him.

"We must bring the fever down and stop the bleeding," Hawk replied in a low voice. "I know what to do about fevers, but I do not know what to do about the bleeding. Birthing wounds are not as easy to deal with as injuries like the one on your head."

Emri reached up and touched the side of his head, wincing as his fingers found the blood-encrusted scab. He had all but forgotten its existence during the trauma of the preceding day.

"I will do what I can," said Hawk, "but I do not know that it will be enough. We need a healer, and I would be most pleased to see another woman."

"We cannot count on finding another tribe," said Emri. "We must do what we can ourselves."

"Then, I will leave you to tend to her and try to cool the heat that fills her body. I will go look for the plants I need to make a tonic."

"But what should I do?" asked Emri in a panic. "I know little of healing."

"There is little enough to do," replied Hawk, his mind already bent to the task of sorting out the many herbs he was familiar with and deciding which would be most appropriate. "Find water, bring it back, and wipe her down with it. We must cool her body until the heat is no more."

"I can do that," Emri said, reassured by the simple instructions and grateful to have something to do.

Grabbing a roasted rabbit from where it lay next to the fire, Hawk slipped through the narrow opening and was gone.

Throughout the long morning, Emri alternately tended the fire, bathed Dawn with rabbit skins dipped in the stream whose course they had climbed, and smoked the remainder of the rabbit carcasses over a secondary fire he had built outside the warren.

Never far from his mind was the sight of the two figures standing on the top of the hill where they had made their last camp. While he doubted that the followers had been able to cross the wide body of water that separated them, he was still concerned.

Time and again, between his duties, he returned to a large tree that clung to the lip of the bluff overlooking the bay and searched the open water for sign of pursuit.

He received little reassurance from the sight of the empty water. He knew full well that if the shaman had sent followers after them, follow they would, unless they believed them to have drowned in the storm. Emri whispered a prayer that it was so.

Toward midday, as broad sunbeams cast thick columns of pale light down through the trees, he was delighted to see Dawn shiver and hear her murmur that she was cold. He covered her lightly with rabbit pelts and soon she fell into a more natural sleep, the dangerous heat having left her body.

Hawk returned by late afternoon, Mosca trotting at his heels. He carried a number of strange bundles and packages wrapped with long grass and tied together with vines. Dropping to the ground beside Emri, he loosed a long breath and closed his eyes for a moment.

"How is she?" he asked at length, as though fearing the answer.

"The heat is gone from her body, though the blood still flows whenever she moves," Emri replied. "She is sleeping now."

"The forest is rich and I have found many things that I sought," said Hawk, sitting up and unwrapping his bundles. "Now we will see if they will work their magic."

He drew a bunch of blood-red roots toward him, obviously broken from the roots of some tree, as well as a number of strips of dark red bark. These he placed on a flat rock and pounded with another rock until they reached a pulpy consistency.

Next, he dug a hole in the damp ground and lined it with a rabbit pelt, fur side down against the earth. Next, he weighted the edges with rocks. When they were secure, he placed half of the pulpy mixture in the hole and then directed Emri to fill it halfway with water he had carried from the stream in another pelt. Then he placed a large number of rocks, each smaller than his closed fist, in the fire. When the rocks were thoroughly heated, he removed them, one at a time with two sticks, and dropped them into the water-filled pit.

The water began to bubble and hiss and roll over and over. After all the stones had been used and the bubbling subsided, Emri saw that the water had turned dark red in color.

"It is done," said Hawk, dipping his finger into the dark brew and tasting it.

Realizing the need, Emri found a soft pine tree and broke off a lower limb of appropriate size. Using his black and red obsidian knife, which thankfully had not been lost during the storm, he whittled a drinking vessel out of the soft wood.

They filled the crude cup with the dark red fluid and slipping into the warren, crouched beside the sleeping girl.

Hawk laid his hand on Dawn's arm gently and her eyes opened. Seeing him, her eyes filled with tears and she smiled tremulously, her mouth trembling like that of a small child.

"Here, Dawn, drink this," Hawk said softly, extending the cup to her.

She stared at him dumbly, as though she did not understand the words, and made no effort to move.

"Please drink it," Emri said, although she had not even turned her eyes toward him. And at the sound of his voice she closed her eyes and turned away from him, the tears flowing silently down her cheeks.

Emri felt the coldness close around his heart and he bowed his head, accepting the blame. Hawk motioned for him to leave, his dark eyes expressing his concern. Knowing that Dawn would not drink with him there, Emri did as he was bid and left the warren.

After a time, Hawk joined him and together they walked into the forest, each heavy with his own thoughts.

"She blames me for the loss of the child," Emri said at length. "She did not want to come. She was afraid but she came because I wished it. I do not think she will ever care for me again."

"Things will change with time," Hawk said, although not denying the truth of Emri's words. "She is sick. She will feel differently when she is well."

"Will she get well?" Emri asked in a low voice.

"She fears that she is sick inside," replied Hawk, not answering Emri's question. "She has told me of a plant that I do not know. I am to search for it. She believes that it will make her better."

"Tell me what it looks like," said Emri, "and I will look too. I do not want her to die."

"We cannot both leave at the same time," said

Hawk, reminding Emri of that which he would have known had his mind not been fogged by emotion.

"She would not be able to defend herself against danger were we both to leave. You should stay, my friend; I will search."

While Hawk was gone, Emri occupied himself with scraping one of the rabbit pelts with the edge of his knife, removing the inner membranes and bits of flesh as well as the fur. Then he stitched both sides together, using thin strips of leather cut from his own tunic.

When it was finished, Emri placed four of the tiny newborn rabbits in the crude sack. Then he wedged the edges of the pelt into six long green sticks that he positioned over the fire, now a bed of glowing coals. He then poured water into the cooking sack and added a few small branches to the coals.

After a while the water began to bubble gently, the heat great enough to cook the rabbits but not cause the water to boil over. The water inside the sack prevented the hide from catching fire.

By the time Hawk returned from his search, a handful of greens dangling from his fist, the air was redolent with a delicate scent of the rabbit broth.

Hawk sniffed the air and nodded to Emri, whose efforts at preparing foodstuffs had never ventured much beyond roasting meats on a stick. Hawk stirred the contents and smiled his approval.

"I have found the greens that she described," Hawk said, lifting the pile of leaves to show Emri, who saw little difference between them and any number of other greens growing on the forest floor.

"I will bring her a cup of this excellent soup and then return to fix these as she bids me. I think you must feed Mosca one of the rabbits, as his own hunting was not as successful as mine."

Emri turned away from the fire and removed one of the rabbits from the fire where it had been drying in the smoke, grateful to Hawk for sparing him from another confrontation with Dawn's unhappiness.

Mosca had no such reservations about his company, and for a short time, Emri and the cub raced through the woods, running and chasing each other and playing games that they devised. But the cat did not play according to the rules, and knowing that Emri carried food, Mosca finished the game quickly by seizing the rabbit and running off to devour it beneath a towering pine.

When they returned to camp, Hawk looked up at them and smiled, a rabbit haunch in his hands and a pile of bones beside him to show that his own meal was nearly done.

"She has drunk the broth and eaten the greens and is sleeping again," he said quietly. "We have done all that we can do, other than speak to the Spirits when their fires light the night sky. If they hear our words, she will be better."

Emri bowed his head to hide his eyes as they filled with water at Hawk's words. He cleared his throat gruffly, and then, turning so that his back was to Hawk, he spoke of the followers and his fear that they would not give up the chase. It was then decided that one of them would remain on watch at all times so as to see their pursuers should they set out from the distant shore.

In his heart, Hawk did not think that such a thing was likely, but Emri had a greater feel for such things just as he himself had a greater affinity for healing herbs, and he held his tongue. In any event, it would give Emri something to do and keep him away from Dawn, allowing her time to bring her emotions, as well as her health, under control.

CHAPTER TWENTY

Broken Tooth and Walks Alone had watched with mixed feelings as .the dark clouds boiled up over the edge of the western horizon.

Broken Tooth was filled with fear for those in the floater. Death, if it had to come, should be swift and their spirits safely sung into the next world. It was not good that they die on the water, their bodies gone from reach and their spirits left to wander the air, forever homeless.

Broken Tooth shivered with the thought of it, glad beyond words that it was not he out on the waters, which were now heaving and jumping like rabbits running before a fire.

The tiny craft, smaller still in the distance, rose and fell, dipping first this way and then that. Broken Tooth felt that it would be but a matter of heartbeats before those it held were thrown into the water and disappeared forever.

At that moment, however, the lead figure turned and looked at him, and even at that distance, somehow he knew that it was Emri. Their eyes locked and Broken Tooth felt, for that brief moment, that the connection was strong enough to draw him back safely to the land. Then he thought of Walks Alone, and the connection was severed as cleanly as though a knife had passed between them.

When next he looked, the craft had vanished, though whether it had been sucked beneath the waters or was merely hidden by the waves he could not tell.

The wind increased, and believing it possible to be blown off the promontory into the waters below, he withdrew from the peak. Shortly afterward, Walks Alone followed.

"Cursed storm," growled Walks Alone as he stalked down to the driftwood dwelling, evidently seeing no irony in taking shelter in the place that their quarry had built. "We must be after them as soon as the storm is done."

Broken Tooth stared at Walks Alone in open-mouthed amazement. "You cannot mean what you say," he said at length. "Surely even you can see that they will die in the storm. No one could live through that. Their bodies are falling through the water by now, and their spirits lost forever. We will never find them. It is time to go home."

Walks Alone looked at him with contempt, his dark eyes hard and flat. "I will believe that they are dead when I see their bodies. You go home, I will follow and avenge the totem by myself." He turned his eyes from Broken Tooth and then left the dwelling, as though unwilling to look upon the man or breathe the same air.

Broken Tooth sat on the cold sand in the darkened dwelling and listened to the wind wail outside. He wrapped his arms around his knees and hugged them to his chest, wishing that he were sitting by the campfire in front of his own dwelling with friends, family and his woman close beside him, telling stories and laughing.

He stared down at the blackened bits of wood, all that remained of Emri's fire, and grieved for his passing. For, in truth, he felt more of a sense of kinship with those whom he had been charged to kill than with Walks Alone.

He tried to picture a fire leaping on the cold coals, and the smiling faces of those who now rested beneath the waters. The vision held for a brief moment and then it vanished, leaving him alone and cold with the ashes.

CHAPTER TWENTY-ONE

The days passed slowly on the plateau as they continued to live beneath the tree trunk waiting for Dawn to regain her strength. Mornings seemed to linger twice as long as usual, and the afternoons dragged by slowly, slowly. The nights were endless.

Emri fretted, knowing that their chances for escape dwindled with every passing day. He had observed the followers attempt two crossings of the wide bay already.

Both attempts had been unsuccessful. Once, a sudden squall had swept across the water and the floater turned back swiftly. The second attempt failed as the tide turned and a series of tall waves bore down on them from the open waters, driving them deep into the heart of the bay.

Emri knew that their luck could not hold forever. Ones so determined would not give up easily, and sooner or later, they would succeed in crossing.

He and Hawk had kept the presence of the followers from Dawn. She was not yet able to travel and there was no reason to alarm her needlessly.

They had discussed their options. If they did not choose to run, they could attack the followers first or even attempt to speak with them.

"I think that we should hide," said Hawk. "They cannot be sure that we are alive. We take care to hide our fire smoke, and few would think to look beneath a tree stump."

"They are not like most others," Emri replied. "Think of the skill it took to follow us this far, through the

fire and down the river and along the coast. They have a
floater as well, and seem to know how to use it. I do not
think that our hiding place would fool them for long.
They would find us and kill us."

"But why do they chase us so?" grumbled Hawk.
"We have never done anything to harm them."

"We killed the tiger," said Emri. "There is no worse
thing we could have done than kill the clan's totem.
Unless it is avenged, its spirit will wreak vengeance on
the tribe. Sickness, famine, death, all will come unless
the totem is avenged."

"But, Emri, we had no choice," protested Hawk.
"We didn't want to kill the tiger. The shaman made it
attack us and we had to fight or die.

"And do you forget that it was sick and dying? If we
had not killed it, it would have perished on its own. We
saved it from greater pain and allowed it to die with
honor."

"I know that and you know that, but I do not think
that we will be able to convince those who follow us,"
said Emri as his eyes swept the bay.

"We could try to talk to them and tell them how it
was," persisted Hawk.

"No, they would not give us a chance to speak," said
Emri. "They will kill us as soon as they have us within
spear range."

"Then, we must stay out of their sight and kill them
first!" Hawk exclaimed, smashing his fist into his open
palm.

"How are we to do that?" asked Emri. "We have
searched the shore where the floater tipped over and
there is no sign of any of our possessions, least of all the
spears. Even if they fell out of the floater before the God
of the Endless Waters swallowed it, they surely rest in
his belly as well. We will never get them back."

"Clubs, we can make clubs," said Hawk. "And we
can make new spears. I will not let them kill me like a
helpless rabbit ready for the food sack!"

"Clubs, yes, we can make clubs," said Emri. "But I
have seen no flint for spearpoints, and as well you

remember, making spear points is not a thing that is
done in haste, at least not for you and I."

"We can fasten your knife to a shaft," said Hawk.
"That would give us one spear until we are able to make
another."

Emri winced at the thought of his precious knife
being turned into a spear whose blade might so easily be
broken, but he could not argue with Hawk's logic; they
needed to be able to protect themselves.

They searched the forest floor and found a piece of
oak that would serve their purpose. Although the proper
length, it was far too wide and not completely straight.

It was a simple matter to drive a wedge into the
wood and thus whittle it down to the proper thickness.
More difficult was the matter of straightening the shaft.
For this, Emri clambered back down the rocky stream-
bed and sorted through the rocks cast up on the stony
shore. Eventually he found what he was looking for, a
smooth piece of sandstone.

A long narrow groove was carefully chiseled in the
sandstone, using the point of a harder rock. The groove
formed a straight line down the center of the rock,
running from edge to edge, the precise shape needed for
the shaft of the spear.

The piece of oak was then fitted into the opening
and drawn through the slot repeatedly until it was
smooth and straight.

The red-and-black-streaked obsidian blade was then
fastened to the shaft with strips of leather cut from
Emri's loincloth.

The balance was not true, owing to the weight of the
knife's handle, which Emri refused to break off, hoping
to one day reclaim the knife for its original purpose.
Thus, the spear would be used more for close stabbing
work than for throwing.

It was determined that Emri would carry the spear,
being both larger and stronger in stature and having had
more experience with the weapon.

But Hawk was unwilling to be caught weaponless,
for even without the threat of the followers, there were
many other dangers in the forest. To this end, he

sacrificed a portion of his own loincloth and fashioned a sling with which he was extremely proficient.

Birds, squirrels, marmots, and rodents found their way into the cooking bag, brought down by Hawk's well-thrown stones. As usual, he rounded out their meals with a wide variety of greens, nuts, and fungus, few of which Emri recognized, all of which he ate.

Within a matter of days, Dawn had recovered enough so that she was able to sit outside and tend to the fire and help Hawk with the cooking.

Although her body was improving, she was quiet and spoke little, initiating few conversations and responding only when spoken to. She seemed listless and uncaring, and even her appearance had changed for the worse; her once-glistening hair was matted and dull, and her eyes were downcast and vague. She made no protest when Emri took her in his arms at night, but neither did she respond.

One day as Emri sat propped against the tree at the edge of the bluff with Mosca sleeping beside him working on a throwing stick, tediously chipping away with a bit of sharp stone, his eye caught a movement on the water. It was the floater! Two figures could be seen clearly as they drove the craft through the water, aiming for the island, just as Emri and Hawk had attempted to do.

Emri searched the sky, hoping for a storm or even a strong wind to stir the waves to great heights, but the sky was a clear, bright blue with no clouds at all. And the waters themselves were flat and calm, heaving slowly and regularly as though the Water God were sleeping.

Startling Mosca into hissing wakefulness, Emri leapt to his feet. The throwing stick was forgotten as he raced back to the warren.

"They are coming!" he cried. "I saw them. They are heading for the island, and if their luck holds, they could be here by nightfall. We must leave!"

"Who is coming and where are we going?" asked Dawn, her eyes showing a spark of their former brightness.

"We are being followed, Dawn," Emri said calmly,

looking her directly in the eye. "Two men. I think Mandris has sent them to kill us. We have been watching for them since we arrived here. They have tried to cross the water twice and failed. I believe that they will make it this time."

"You have stayed here because of me," said Dawn, realizing all in spite of Emri's carefully chosen words. "You could have been far from here, had you not waited. Why did you not tell me?"

"You were not well enough to travel," replied Hawk, breaking into the conversation and hoping to divert tension. "And we thought that we could defend ourselves. After all, are we not brothers to the lion?"

"Even brothers to the lion know when it is time to fight and when it is time to go," said Dawn, still holding Emri's gaze. And to Emri's great relief, he saw her draw herself up tall and her head take on its familiar tilt, full of resolve and proud daring. He smiled at her as the warmth of joy spread through his body. Her eyes still held his gaze, and slowly, nodding as though in understanding and forgiveness of all that had transpired, she smiled back.

"Come," she said, "we have spent more than enough time in this place. Brothers to the lion do not belong in a rabbit warren; it is time for us to go."

They gathered the few possessions that remained to them and then did their best to obliterate all signs of their encampment. They placed everything that they had used, including the remains of the fire, inside the warren and then shoveled dirt on top of it and covered the earth with leaves and needles. When they were finished, it appeared much as they had found it. They retreated into the forest, brushing out their tracks as they went.

Dawn had not fully regained her strength, but she refused to admit that she was tired, driving them on long after they would have stopped.

They camped for the night, high in the branches of an immense pine, making no fire and eating cold smoked rabbit. Their sleep was uneasy and interrupted by frequent checks of the ground below, but other than an

owl whose eerie cries sent chills down their backs, there
was no sign or sound of pursuit.

The land changed rapidly, growing more and more
foreign to them with every passing day. The smaller
softwoods began to disappear, replaced by the larger and
more impressive hardwoods and equally immense pines,
often towering so high that their crowns could not be
seen.

Great white birds, as large as humans with long,
thin, trailing legs, made their nests in the tops of these
giant trees. Each nest was as big as a human dwelling,
and was constructed of large sticks and limbs of trees.

The air grew more moist, and cooler as well; often
they could see their breath steam in the crisp mornings
and nights. Mist frequently hung about them, unmoving, and their bodies gleamed with moisture as they
passed through it.

Ferns and thick clumps of moss grew in profusion
and it was difficult to pass without trampling it underfoot, leaving a clear sign for those who followed. They
were painstaking in their efforts to avoid leaving prints,
but much of their effort was undone by Mosca, who
neither understood nor cared.

Mosca delighted in the new landscape, gamboling
about as though he were still a young cub, chasing
brilliantly hued butterflies and red squirrels who chas-
tised him from the safety of the trees, screaming "*chuh,
chuh, chuh,*" invectives that caused him to leap and
pounce and growl as though replying in kind.

The wonder of the changing land removed much of
the sting from their flight. Each discovery of a new plant
or tree or brightly colored salamander brought happy
exclamations to their lips, and Emri was overjoyed at the
changes that were occurring in Dawn as she slowly
regained her normal manner.

And still there was no sign of the followers. No sign
of smoke, no sound of pursuit. Emri began to hope that
the follower's voyage might have ended in failure and
that he and his companions would escape the long arm of
the shaman.

The snow- and ice-covered peaks of the mountains
had long been within sight, but now they drew closer.

Visible at all times to the east, and occasionally to the north, they beckoned to Emri like a beacon. The Endless Waters remained on their left, the sound of the waves on the rocks, a constant whisper like the sighing of wind in the treetops.

Strangest of all was the sight of ice floating in the water. Most were small chunks, no larger than a human dwelling, that bobbed up and down and frequently drifted in to shore where they were soon ground to bits on the sand and rocks. Others, however, were not so small and sailed by, awe-inspiring in size, glinting blue-white in the bright sun. The water beasts delighted in these large floes of ice, leaping up out of the water onto their wide shelves and sprawling on their backs, flippers spread wide, safe from the biters that prowled the waters in large numbers. The biters' sharp fins could often be seen cutting through the waters, and Emri was glad that they were no longer traveling in the floater.

Emri's heart raced with excitement as the icy peaks drew near. He did not know why the sight of them brought him such pleasure, but he often lay awake at night, long after his tired body begged him for the relief of sleep, and wondered what he would find when they reached the land of ice and snow.

He knew the old tales by heart, knew that it was from this same land of perpetual cold that his own ancestors had come, traveling from yet another land that lay still further beyond. He tried to vision what these people would look like. Would they look the same as the people of his clan, or would they be different as Toads and Tigers were different.

He tried to imagine the animals, and wondered if they would be the same or stranger than anything he had ever seen. These thoughts and many others filled his mind both waking and sleeping, and drew him on like a lodestone, more effective than the thought of the followers behind.

Hawk, ever impressionable and more than willing to share Emri's dream, discussed the possibilities of what they might find, his own passion growing as they drew nearer to the mysterious peaks.

The land changed still further as they continued to push north. The hemlocks and cedars and oaks had all but vanished, replaced almost entirely by a vast conifer forest that stretched on as far as the eye could see. Mountains rose to the right of them, but these they did not climb, remaining on the slopes beside the Endless Waters.

The air had grown even cooler and the nights were undeniably chill. There was often frost on the ground when they wakened in the morning, and light blankets of ice bridged the streams. They crossed the small streams and the larger rivers by various means. Draining from the ice caps in the higher elevations, the rivers were often a strange milky white in color.

Using slings, clubs, and snares, they succeeded in adding to their supply of meat and pelts. Once, they found a large stag caught between two trees, his immense rack of antlers wedged so firmly that he was unable to free himself. Dodging his sharp hooves and ignoring his enraged bellows, they bombarded him with stones until they crushed his skull and he died.

They fell upon the stag as though it were a gift from the Gods. Aside from the meat, which they ate in great quantities, they used nearly every bit of the immense beast to replace their vanished possessions.

The hide was expertly stripped from the carcass, which weighed more than all three of them combined. The hide was then pegged to the ground, fur side down so that Dawn might scrape the inner surface with a sharp stone, carefully removing every bit of fat, flesh, and inner membrane.

Once the surface was cleaned, she rubbed it with a mixture of the stag's brains and wood ashes, working it into the pores of the hide to cure it. Later, after the hide had cured, she would pound it between two smooth rocks to make it pliable so that it could be worked.

The hooves were boiled over a long slow fire until they softened and became viscous, turning into a gluey substance that would hold or mend a wide variety of materials from hide to stone. This glue was poured into gourds that they had been fortunate enough to find in the lower forest.

The sinews were drawn out of the flesh and hung over branches of trees to dry. After they dried, the fibers would be carefully separated and rolled into tiny bundles that would later be used for sewing.

Needles would be made from the long thin leg bones of a bird. These precious needles would be kept from loss by stringing a thread through a hole in the base, and were worn around Dawn's neck at all times.

The heavier leg bones of the stag would be used as clubs, and the antlers themselves would be worked into knives, flint flakers, leather awls, wedges, pegs, and a variety of other tools. When they were done, nothing was left of the stag save bones. Even those had been cracked in two and the marrow extracted. What little remained would soon be devoured by foxes, wolves, and other predators.

Burdened by the heavy meat, their progress was slower than Emri wished. But he realized that they did not know what lay ahead. Food might be very difficult to find in the Cold Lands. Also, with food at hand, it was not necessary to stop and hunt for their every meal, nor did they need to set snares each night when their bodies cried out for sleep.

One thought turned round and round in their minds. Not once since they left the Toad camps had they seen another human being other than the followers. Emri had expected to find other tribes with whom they might speak and eventually join. Though they had watched for smoke plumes, they had seen no fire other than their own.

Food was not the problem. Long-neck grazers and fleet-footed little horses had been abundant, mingling freely with wooly bison and antelope.

Tuskers had been seen, as well as the great sloths and slow-moving, waddling horny-backs. Fat rabbits abounded in the moist forests, as did huge herds of deer.

Deer and elk were present now and in such numbers that they no longer feared the followers, for the hooves of the herds, all moving slowly south, would obliterate all signs of their passing.

The deer were streaming toward them out of the north. At first it had been no more than a trickle, but now the herds were so vast that it was sometimes hard to see where one herd left off and another began.

At first they had been overwhelmed by the sheer numbers of the deer; never had any of them seen anything like this. They had thought to kill another deer, and readied their clubs and stones, but then Emri lowered his arm and halted their aim. There was no purpose in killing so large an animal. They did not need the meat and could not carry it, weighted down as they were.

In the end, they made their way through the herds, often passing so close that they could have reached out and touched the wide-eyed females and skittering fawns who danced by on improbably long thin legs.

The deer streamed south in a continuous river of flesh, followed in turn by dire wolves, fox, and coyote. The deer themselves were curiously without fear, scarcely taking note of the humans who stood in their path. So heavy was the press from those who followed that they could not have stopped had they wished to do so.

Quite a different story were the stags who led the herds, and those without herds who sought to gain them. These, with their wide-spread racks of many-pronged antlers, were creatures best left alone. Normally complacent creatures for most of the year, as the days passed from Warm Time into the high color of Leaf Fall, the stags entered the mating season and saw danger in every direction as the madness of rut seized their minds.

Once, Mosca, unable to avail himself of Emri and Hawk's knowledge, had flung himself at a small fawn, pouncing on its hindquarters and bringing it down with his sheer weight. Before the cat could wrap his front paws around the fawn and bite through the jugular or sever the neck, the tiny creature staggered to its feet and ran bleating through the herd, blood streaming down its back.

Its piteous cries attracted the attention of a young

stag, not even one who led the herd, but one who hoped to steal or attract enough does to start his own herd. Eyes ringed with white, it placed itself between the startled cat and the frantic fawn, lowering its head and pawing the ground. Unfortunately for Mosca, he was unimpressed by this most unusual deerlike behavior and he slunk forward, thinking to catch the deer off guard and leap for its neck.

The stag gave him no opportunity to do so, for it lowered its head still further, pointing the rack of sharp-tipped horns directly at Mosca, and ran toward him at full speed.

Emri, Hawk, and Dawn had been calling to the cat, hoping to draw him away before the stag charged. His intentions were all too clear to them: he intended to impale the cat on his horns and then trample him into the ground.

But Mosca ignored them completely, as did the stag, and it was only as the stag thundered toward him, his great weight shaking the earth, that Mosca realized his danger and ran for the safety of a tree.

The stag pursued him. Round and round the trees they ran, the stag hooking his horns at the cat's retreating tail, bellowing out his fury.

Finally, he treed the cat, and so great was his rage that he drove his horns into the trunk time and again, shaking the tree with the violence of his blows. Unable to dislodge the cat, the stag came looking for another victim. It galloped around the tree and through the ferns with foam dripping from his nostrils and open mouth.

The stag's anger seemed to increase with the loss of the cat and, one after the other, he chased Emri, Dawn, and Hawk until all of them were forced to climb trees to avoid its murderous hooves and horns.

Unwilling to declare defeat, the stag remained beneath the trees, rocking first one then another with heavy battering blows.

It was dark and they were all cold, hungry, and thirsty before the stag departed, still blowing and snorting and pawing the ground.

"Do you think he's really gone?" asked Hawk calling from his perch. "Is it safe to come down?"

"I don't know," replied Emri. "I can't see him anywhere, but that doesn't mean that he can't see us. Maybe he's just out of sight, waiting for us to give up and come down so he can get us."

"I think we should stay where we are," said Dawn. "He could be anywhere."

"Ho!" cried Hawk, "I am brother to the lion! I do not fear the deer!" But despite his brave words, Hawk remained in the tree along with the rest of them, until the forest brightened with the pale light of morning, the long hours unrelieved by any sound but that of Mosca's unhappy bawling.

When finally they were able to see that the stag had indeed given up his furious offense, they discovered that Mosca had climbed far up into the heights of a great pine and would not come down.

At first it seemed humorous, but then as the cub continued to bawl, refusing to release the trunk of the tree, they began to lose their humor. They tempted him with bits of meat and threatened him with closed fists, but nothing caused him to come down. At last, Emri was forced to climb the tree, grab him by the nape of the neck and guide him forcefully back to earth.

From that time, Mosca was careful to search the air for the scent of stags before chasing any more deer. Even then he broke off his attack after a few exuberant bounds, reserving his hunting for rabbits and squirrels who did not fight back.

CHAPTER TWENTY-TWO

Walks Alone was not happy. They had crossed the big water, it was true, quartering first to the island, which had nearly been the end of them. The island—an immense expanse of rock sticking up out of the water like the humped back of a snapping turtle—was surrounded by huge sharp rocks.

The floater had been driven onto the rocky coast in spite of all their efforts to stay clear. The tall waves drove them relentlessly onto the rocks, which pierced the floater in as many places as a man had fingers and more.

The floater quickly filled with water. Only the fact that they were able to cling to the rocks and pull themselves and the stricken floater to shore saved them from being swallowed by the Water God.

Broken Tooth had been badly frightened at their brush with death and had wondered aloud whether the God of the Waters would feel cheated and search for them when next they braved the waters.

The thought alarmed Walks Alone, and though he jeered at Broken Tooth when he spoke, he did not stop him from making an offering to the Water God. In the night, after Broken tooth had gone to sleep, he too made an offering of his own.

The island was an inhospitable place, offering no shelter other than thin bent trees that did little to break the constant wind. Broken Tooth gathered bits of wood that had been driven onto the rocks and built a lean-to using a small tree for the central support.

It was crudely done, but green branches laced through the spaces closed it off more effectively, and

gave them some protection from the wind. Their fire-
starting coal, carried as was Emri's in the safety of a
freshwater clamshell, had been crushed in the rough
landing and they were forced to start a fire by hand.

Building the shelter, starting the fire, and spearing a
fish for a meal took up all of the remaining day. Broken
Tooth closed his eyes and slept as soon as his belly was
filled, curling up as close to the fire as possible.

Walks Alone, unable to sleep—as usual—curled his
lip at Broken Tooth's sloth, but, in truth, a part of him
envied the man for his ability to put aside that which he
could do nothing about. He was not tormented by
obsessions that drove him on long after other men
stopped.

Briefly, Walks Alone wondered what it would be like
to be such a man. Then he thrust the thought from him,
as though even the thought were somehow improper, a
sign of weakness.

He had not thought that the trip would take so long.
The island had seemed reachable. He had thought that
they would make landfall, then carry the floater to the far
end of the island and strike out for the distant shore.

He walked to the waterline and hunkered down,
staring across at where he imagined the land to be,
where he knew his quarry lay. At some point, he had
stopped thinking of them as individuals. They were no
longer people; as in a hunt, they had become the quarry.

He cast a quick glance up at the sky and was
relieved to note that it was overcast with heavy clouds.
He was glad that the ancestors were not able to see his
failure, and he vowed that by the next nightfall they
would have achieved the mainland and located their
quarry.

But the next day was rainy and overcast as well, and
the water was overlaid by a heavy mist that did not lift
until midafternoon, when the current was clearly running away from the land. Even if the floater had been
whole, it would have been impossible to leave.

But the floater was not whole. They quickly determined it could not be repaired by sewing, for the water
seeped in the holes left by the needle. It was apparent

that some other method was needed if the floater were ever to ride the waves again.

At length, Broken Tooth suggested glue, but none of the usual materials were available to them; there were no resinous pine trees on the island, nor were there any large animals with hooves.

They might have been forced to remain there forever if Broken Tooth had not remembered hearing someone mention that glue could be made out of fish. Unfortunately, he had only heard a snatch of the conversation and did not know what part of the fish was used, or how it was done.

Thus began a long and frustrating period. They used lines made of sinew and precious hooks fashioned out of stone and horn to catch the fish. Once caught, they experimented, preparing the fish in a variety of ways, all of which smelled and none of which worked.

They boiled the flesh till it disintegrated, pounded it with rocks while raw, and spread it on the hide and allowed it to dry. They separated the fish skins and plastered them to the hide. They tried boiling the skins and skimming off the oil that rose to the surface, but none of those methods worked either.

At long last, after Broken Tooth had given up, and sat looking glumly at the water, and wondering if he would ever see his woman again, Walks Alone found the answer.

He had carefully separated all the flesh and skin from a large fish, keeping only the skull, scales, and bones. These he pounded into a smooth pulp and then cooked it slowly over a low fire. This process yielded a thin, clear yellow liquid. Once strained through a porous inner membrane of tree bark to remove the bits of fish solids that remained, the yellow liquid bonded readily to the hide. Walks Alone had made glue.

Using this glue and bits of hide cut from their own clothing, they patched the floater. On the morning of the eighth day, they launched the floater and headed for the distant shore.

CHAPTER TWENTY-THREE

The last of the great herds had passed them days ago. Now only the stragglers—and the wolves and coyotes who followed them—remained. These creatures, either sick, old, or delayed by late-born calves, were wide-eyed and vigilant as they watched the confident predators who haunted their heels. Few of them would ever rejoin the safety of the herds.

The days were colder now, yet still quite pleasant while the sun was shining. The trees were fewer in number, with wide spaces between them, the tall firs giving way to white-barked birches and red-hued fragrant cedars.

The snow- and ice-capped peaks were clearly visible, rising to the right and ahead of them in a solid wall. They were beautiful and awesome; they had about them a sense of power, as though they were the home of Gods.

When the sun struck the peaks and the flow of ice that poured down the slopes, there were brilliant flashes of red and gold, as though the Sun God were throwing spears of fire.

Before and after the sun crested the peaks, the fire dimmed to deep purple and blue, shades found only in the wing of a bird or a flower's petals. In the full of the day when the sun rode high overhead, the ice glittered and sparkled like the light on dancing water, so bright that it hurt one's eyes to look at it.

The beauty of the ice was so magnificent that it brought an ache to Emri's chest. All of his earlier doubts and fears had vanished. He felt a great peace in his heart, as though the Gods had called to him and he had answered with his presence. He knew that he had been right to come.

"It will be all right now," he told the others. "The Gods wished for us to come, they will provide for us. You will see. They will send us a sign, telling us what to do."

Hawk and Dawn, less certain than Emri, glanced at each other, then cast their eyes down, unwilling for Emri to see their doubt.

But from that moment on, it seemed as though Emri had been right. Perfect campsites appeared each night, campsites with clear-running water and rocks or groves of trees to provide shelter and an abundance of firewood in a land where trees had suddenly become scarce.

Game appeared as well, large fat rabbits with thick white pelts, who sat wide-eyed and trusting as though they had never been hunted. Large black berries, as big as their thumbs and bursting with juice and flavor, hung heavy amid tangles of thorny vines.

Dawn cried aloud with pleasure when first she saw them, and she set them all to gathering the fruit and spreading it out on rocks to dry in the sun. Nor would she leave, despite their grumbling, until she had filled a large rabbit-skin pouch to the top with the dried fruit.

She knew that the fruit would be as precious as meat throughout the long hard months of Cold Time. It could be used in a wide variety of ways, from soups to medicinal drinks, its sweet flavor recalling the glorious days of warmth while they were locked in the icy grip of Cold Time.

When the pouch could hold no more, Dawn agreed to leave, although she would have been more than happy to have stayed. But the call was strong upon Emri. His eyes were drawn again and again to the glistening peaks and his manner was distracted, as though only part of him were present.

The last of the trees were left behind as they advanced toward the bright ice. Slender willows and low bushes were all that remained of the great forests. Tough, ground-hugging grasses and sedges carpeted the earth. Icy streams cut through the land, running thick and opaque, tumbling hurriedly down from the peaks to the east seemingly anxious to pour themselves into the vast body of the Endless Waters.

One bright chill day they came to a broad stream that was quite different from the clouded white torrents they had come to expect. This stream flowed clear and it was possible to see all the way to the bottom.

While searching for a crossing, Emri had immediately noticed something strange. The water was choked with fish the length and width of his arm, all swimming upstream. Their bodies were silver, flushed with red, and their heads were ugly with gaping eyes, gasping mouths and hooked jaws.

Never having seen such a mass of fish gathered together at one time, Emri speared one and pulled it from the stream, its weight dragging against the spear. So heavy was the fish and so fiercely did it fight that Emri fell back on the ground, still holding the spear. Only when the fish was clubbed with a stone did it cease its struggle.

The flesh was bright red and firm and strong of taste. None of them had ever eaten anything like it before. So plentiful were these fish that Hawk demanded that they stay long enough to catch and smoke a supply. Dawn, ever concerned about food, was in agreement and Emri could not refuse.

They had no trouble catching the fish, for their numbers appeared to be endless and the stream seemed to hold more fish than water. The surface of the water was roiled with their movement as they fought their way upstream, even slithering over rocks in places where their passage was blocked, and at times their bodies rose completely out of the water. It was a simple matter to spear them and soon they had three large mounds of the slippery silver fish.

Mosca enjoyed the fishing even more than did the humans, dancing back and forth on the bank, clawing fish out of the water and then pouncing on them with great excitement. He seldom ate them, the fun being in the catching. Often he rolled in fish that had succumbed to the journey and lay rotting at the water's edge.

Soon, the cat was so rank that they refused to allow him to join them at the fire, throwing rocks and pebbles at him when he came close, and calling him names. He contented himself with lying just outside the ring of firelight, where the smell still gagged them but he himself was out of their reach.

They prepared the fish by slitting them and removing the entrails. Dawn gathered dried cakes of dung left by the passing herds and built fires. She then suspended the fish above the smoke on willow racks where they remained until they were thoroughly smoked.

The flesh, while carrying the taste of smoke, still retained a delicate flavor that, if possible, was an improvement over the freshly roasted fish. All were happy with the results. The fish were carefully packed inside three large rabbit-skin pouches, each long enough to drape across the shoulders and secured by straps cut from the hide of the stag.

Shortly before dawn on the final night of their stay, they were awakened by the sound of Mosca screaming. They came awake instantly, each of them familiar with the range of the cat's noises and recognizing this as a cry of fear and warning.

They scrambled from their furskins, reaching for their spears and clubs. And in the pale, watery gray light that comes before the true dawn they saw a shambling mountainous shape advancing on the cat.

Mosca was huddled into himself, retreating backward, snarling and hissing and squalling loudly, making occasional feints with his front paws even though he was hopelessly outclassed.

Emri's heart sank as he recognized the attacker as a great black bear—not the larger cave bear, but equally ferocious with powerful teeth and claws as long and sharp as those of the cat.

Emri's heart pounded as he tried desperately to think of a plan, but there was nowhere for Mosca or them to go. There were no trees to climb and there was nowhere to hide on the flat landscape. Their puny weapons could not hope to kill or even seriously wound the bear. Killing a bear required many, many men with

long, keen-edged spears. Stones were useless, as they
would do nothing but enrage the fierce carnivore. Nor
could they outrun him.

The bear was still stalking toward Mosca, the fur on
his humped neck standing up in spiky ridges. His head
was down low, swaying back and forth, and a deep
moaning sound issued from his snarling lips.

Mosca was arched into a tight bow, literally dancing
on the tips of his toes, skidding sideways and yowling an
eerie cry. His fur stood up all over his body, making him
appear twice his normal size, and his ears were pasted
back flat against his head.

The bear was backing Mosca down toward the
stream. Emri did not know what would happen when
they reached the water, for while the cat did not mind
playing along the edges, he disliked water with a
passion, and all the more since the trip in the floater.

When they reached the water's edge, Mosca
crouched down nearly flat to the ground and hissed. The
hissing had absolutely no effect on the bear and he
swatted at the cat. Mosca leaped into the air, a feat that
Emri would have thought impossible, given the cat's
position, and came down hissing, spitting, and screaming all at the same time. He landed running with the
bear in pursuit, running upstream, away from the camp.

They lost no time in gathering their possessions and
heading in the opposite direction. Fortunately, Dawn
had packed all of the fish away in anticipation of their
departure. All that remained was the most recent catch
and these they left, feeling that their lives were of more
value than a few dried fish.

As they hurried away into the foggy dawn, Emri
listened for sounds of combat, but there was nothing to
be heard. He prayed to the Gods that Mosca had
escaped, for there was nothing more frightening than an
angry bear. The odds were with the cat, for though the
bear was four times Mosca's size, it was built for power
rather than speed. And as every child knew, you couldn't
be killed if you couldn't be caught.

They barely noticed the frigid waters of the stream
as they crossed at a narrow ford studded with large

rocks, so grateful were they at escaping the bear. If Mosca had not been there to draw the bear's attention, the animal would be feeding on one of them now. Emri shuddered at the thought and hurried on, praying to his ancestors to keep the cat safe.

CHAPTER TWENTY-FOUR

Not wanting to abandon Mosca, they fled only a short distance to a high point of land that was strewn with a dense layer of fist-sized stones. They reasoned that if the bear appeared, they would be able to drive it off with a constant rain of rocks. But the bear did not appear, nor did Mosca.

They remained on the rocky rise until the sun burned off the heavy layer of fog that blanketed the land each night. They could see the stream clearly and there was no sign of either animal. As the morning wore on, Emri became more and more restless.

"I must go and find what has happened to Mosca," he said at last. Dawn's arguments did nothing to dissuade him. He refused to allow Hawk to accompany him, arguing that if he were to fall to the bear, one more set of hands would do little good and would leave Dawn alone. Arming himself with both spear and club, he set off in search of the cat.

His spirits plummeted as he scouted their former campsite, seeing nothing but a flock of black birds plundering their fish. Treading lightly, he tracked the prints of both cat and bear along the edge of the stream.

The tracks were easy to follow, for the bear's great weight left deep impressions in the damp soil. Also visible were the claw marks of the cat as its hind paws dug in for greater traction. Emri continued on, scanning the ground ahead of him fearfully, more than half expecting to see the torn carcass of the cat lying dead at every step.

But it was the bear he saw first, rising out of the water directly ahead of him, like some huge living rock. There were no signs of battle on the thick pelt that rippled and shone in the sunlight. It stood placidly in midstream, water lapping at its fat belly as it probed beneath the surface for the silver fish.

Even as Emri watched in astonishment, the bear hooked one of the immense fish and flung it onto the bank. It turned and lumbered after the fish, its heavy body throwing up sheets of water.

On the bank it seized the flapping fish in its powerful jaws and severed the backbone with one crunch. Moaning happily, it sank to the ground holding the fish in its front paws, and like a child held a stick when the sweetsap was rising, it began to devour it.

Emri stood still as a rock as the wind suddenly switched direction and blew his scent directly toward the bear. But the bear paid him no heed, all of his interest being focused on the fish.

After a time, the bear finished eating, waddled back into the stream, and began fishing for another.

Emri seized the chance to skirt the immense creature and hurry away, now following the tracks of the cat alone.

He found Mosca curled up atop a tall rock, sound alseep in the warm sunlight, apparently unharmed. Emri felt a great rush of relief at the sight of the cat, for he had certainly feared the worst.

Looking down on the sleeping cat, he realized how much Mosca meant to him. He regarded Mosca, not so much as an animal, but almost as he would a younger brother. He found himself wondering, not for the first time, if Mosca were more than he seemed, perhaps a spirit sent to him by his dead father, to guide him in his life. Such things had been known to happen, through usually only in visions.

Mosca opened his eyes and yawned shrilly stretching his paws out on the rock, extending the long curved claws.

"Ho, brother, it is good that you are safe," Emri said

softly. "We were much worried for you. Come, let us go, before the bear tires of fish and comes searching for us."

Mosca blinked, his amber eyes shining gold in the sunlight, and after a lick or two to his hind leg and short stubby tail, the cat leaped down from the rock and sat at Emri's feet.

Emri scratched the top of Mosca's head and behind his tufted ears, happy to feel the heavy weight against his leg and the deep rumbling in the cat's chest once more.

They crossed the icy torrent at the nearest ford, enduring the wider and deeper breadth of the stream rather than risk encountering the bear a second time. And as they struck out on an angle calculated to bring them to the rise where Hawk and Dawn awaited them, they saw several more bears gathered at the stream. It was evident that they had stumbled on a favorite feeding spot of the dangerous animals.

Emri wondered briefly if the stream were always filled with the strange silver fish or if it were a yearly occurrence like the traveling of the birds. If so, they were lucky to have escaped with only a scare, and would have to be on their guard against other bears.

It was a wise decision, for they were forced to take evasive action a number of times during the days ahead. Bears were everywhere, prowling the open land, stuffing their bellies with the sweet black berries that appeared in low, protected spots, and lining the banks of every clear-running stream.

They were forced to make cold camps, eating the smoked fish, meat, and dried berries, for to have lit a fire would have been too risky, attracting bears to them like insects to carrion.

There was only one good thing that arose from the massive influx of bears. One evening as they made their way across yet another stream, they found the body of a nearly full-grown female bear half submerged in the icy waters.

It was clear from the terrible wounds around the head, neck, and shoulders of the animal that it had been killed in a fight with another bear, perhaps in a dispute over fishing rights. The bear's head lolled at an unnatural angle, its neck broken, clear evidence of the opponent's great strength.

Frightened as they were of encountering the victor, the heavy pelt was too great a prize to leave. After a hurried discussion, they agreed to skin the bear, hoping to strip the hide from the carcass and be gone before they were discovered.

It was a long night. Temperatures dipped even lower than usual and frost appeared on the ground around them. A heavy mist swirled above the stream, the sort that unfriendly spirits were known to inhabit.

But the spirits, if any, must have been friendly, for the three travelers were not troubled. Their hands and feet were numb and aching long before morning as they struggled to free the pelt from the great beast in the frigid stream. So heavy was the creature that it was totally impossible for them to move the body onto dry land, and they were forced to work in the black icy water.

They finished the difficult chore shortly before dawn, just as the birds began to murmur sleepy calls that drifted over the land like homeless spirits. The pelt, half sodden with water, was too heavy for Dawn to lift, and Hawk rolled it into a great bundle and tied it on his own shoulders.

Emri felt the edge of his obsidian blade, which had been used to separate the hide from the flesh, and knew that it would have to be sharpened, for it had been blunted against the tough hide and lost its keen edge.

In addition to the thick pelt, they removed all four paws, complete with the great curved claws, the four long canine teeth, and the thick layer of yellow fat. This fat, which was heaviest now after Warm Time, was, if anything, as valuable as the pelt, and would be used as the base for numerous healing unguents and medicinal salves. Having no pouch to place it in, the fat was simply rolled in the hide that had covered it in life.

Other than a haunch for themselves and a foreleg for Mosca, who had growled his displeasure throughout the night, they took no other meat. They were burdened greatly as it was, and bear meat had a heavy, rank taste that lingered long on the tongue.

"The ancestors surely guided our feet," Dawn said as they trudged away from the stream. "This one will keep us warm throughout Cold Time and its fat will soothe our hurts. My own mother has often spoken of her desire to possess such a pelt; never did I think to own one myself." Then her words seemed to dwindle away and she fell silent, no doubt sorrowing as she thought of her mother, whom she might never see again.

"Look you for a safe place to shelter," Emri said brusquely, pretending not to notice her sorrow. "We must find a place where we will be safe from this one's brothers as we sleep."

Mention of their own needs brought Dawn's attention back to the present. Unfortunately, the land had become even more barren than before.

Trees were now a thing of the past; alders, white-skinned birch, and even willows were now gone from the landscape. Other than rocks, boulders, and the constant crisscross of streams making their way to the Endless Waters, low-lying tough grass, thick sedges, and a variety of moss and lichen were all that clothed the land.

Eventually, driven by exhaustion and hunger, they made their way to the top of a small hill that rose above the rolling landscape, crowned by a large rock outcrop. Here they made their camp and, after swallowing a few mouthfuls of food, rolled themselves up in their furskins and fell asleep instantly.

Emri alone remained awake, for it had been decided that while they traversed the territory of the bears, one of them would stay on guard at all times.

Emri climbed to the top of the outcrop, a chunk of dried, smoked deer meat in his hand and a sliver of ice pried from a crevice in the rock to salve his thirst.

He sought out the horizon to the south, searching for a sign of pursuit either human or bear, but there was nothing, no movement other than the white birds of the water wheeling and dipping over the land as they did at dawn and dusk every day.

Next he turned his eyes to the east and watched as

the sun's first rays caressed the peaks, first crimson then
scarlet, then magenta and gold. Each color was more
radiant than the last, filling his heart to bursting, so
intense was the splendor.

At last the sun crested the peaks and sent its rays
cascading down the slopes and flooding onto the barren
land below, bestowing beauty on everything it touched.
Curtains of mist twisted and swirled, draped in delicate
rainbows. Each drop of dew on each blade of grass was
tipped with fire so bright that Emri was forced to close
his eyes.

The waters to the west, heavy and sluggish with ice,
seemed to dance in the light, rays of sunlight bouncing
off their surfaces and reflecting back to the shore in
sparkling swathes of brilliance.

So bedazzled was Emri, so bemused by the brilliant
display of light, that for a time he did not realize what he
was seeing. There, there in the north, still swaddled in
curling mists, were plumes of smoke rising high into the
cold blue sky, like signals to the Gods.

For long heartbeats he stared at the plumes,
assuring himself that they were not merely mist, nor
visions that he had conjured up of longing.

Once satisfied that the smoke was real, he leaned on
his spear and watched as it filled the sky, knowing that
what they had sought for so long had come to them at
last.

CHAPTER TWENTY-FIVE

Broken Tooth and Walks Alone drove the floater through the water with powerful thrusts, aiming for the distant headland. But the currents were contrary and fought their every move. When at last they were able to bring their craft to shore, it was with the aid of the evening tide, which bore them relentlessly up into the mouth of the wide bay. Only after it slackened and began to drift back out were they able to break free of its grip and make landfall.

The shoreline was a mass of tumbled rocks that defied easy access to the land above. They made an uneasy camp on the cold, rocky beach and set out early the next morning.

It was Walks Alone who spotted the wreckage of the floater hanging limp and broken, high in the rocks where it had been cast and then abandoned by the terrible storm. It lay shattered like a broken bird, trodden into the earth, never to rise again.

They landed their own craft carefully, beaching it carefully between the rocks, and discovered that the floater still held all of the enemy's possessions.

They examined the obsidian spear points with interest, exclaiming over their keen edges and dividing them reluctantly. The food was saturated with salt water, inedible, was discarded to the delight of the inquisitive white birds who circled above them, filling the air with their harsh cries. Dawn's packets of possessions they stowed among their own, Broken Tooth in particular was especially grateful for the healing herbs and unguents.

Careful observation showed them the only spot the

enemy might have gained access to the land. Shelving their floater high on the rocks, out of reach of the highest waves, they made their way up the rock-choked gorge and entered the silent forest.

Despite Emri and Hawk's efforts, it was not hard to locate the warren that had been their hideout. Nor was it difficult to ascertain that they had continued their voyage on foot. Since their floater had been destroyed, there was really no other alternative.

After a short discussion, it was decided that they would retrieve their own floater and hide it in the trees, safe from prowling beasts until their return. Never once did Walks Alone doubt that they, or at least he, would return.

Shouldering their packs, spears, and knives at the ready, they set off in search of the enemy.

CHAPTER TWENTY-SIX

When the sun reached the roof of the sky and hesitated, as though unwilling to begin the long descent that would end once again in its nightly death, Emri wakened Hawk and Dawn. Wordlessly he pointed out the plumes of smoke, which had increased in number and were clearly drawn against the sky.

Hawk turned to Emri with eyes bright with excitement. "You were right, my friend. We have found others as you said we would. I feel in my heart that our steps were guided to this spot. All will be well from this time forward."

Dawn looked at Emri and smiled. Her heart still ached at the loss of the child, but she had ceased holding Emri responsible, for it had been her own action, lying with him on the furskin without benefit of clan approval or ritual, that had set all later events in motion.

Emri had more than proved himself, guiding them to this spot in relative safety through dangerous and unknown lands. In spite of the child, she did not regret her decision to follow Emri wherever he might lead.

They neatened themselves as best they were able, and combed and braided their hair, fastening it with strips of leather threaded through shells they had gathered on the shore. Then, shouldering their packs, they set off toward the distant fires.

The land rose and fell beneath their feet in a series of gentle crenellations, rises of land separated by streams of opaque water flowing from the mountains of ice to the east. These mountains had drawn closer and closer to the Endless Waters the further north they travelled, and now they lay no more than one day's march distant.

These gentle hills continued to hide the source of the fires from them, for it always seemed that there was another rise higher than the one they climbed between them and the final view. Also, curiously, there seemed to be a veil of mist concealing that which they most desired to see.

As the afternoon wore on, the sun beat down on their heads, warming them in spite of the cold rising from the semifrozen land. Then, suddenly, unexpectedly, cresting yet another hill they came across a broad spit of snow and ice that pushed its way west from the bulk of the mountain that rose behind it and seemed to reach out for the Endless Waters that lay just beyond.

The mountain itself rose steeply behind the finger of ice, a pale, watery shade of blue-white that seemed to blend into the sky. Emri felt that if he blinked, it might disappear forever, so insubstantial did it appear.

The bulk of the mountain, which was itself made of ice, lay to the east of the Endless Waters and curved around to the north as well, paralleling the shore and stretching away as far as the eye could see with a slim margin of land between it and the ice-choked waters.

But just beyond the lobe of ice, nestled improbably in a curve of land lay the village they had been seeking, the fires still rising to the sky like signals.

They stood on the crest of the cold spit and stared down at the scene in stunned silence, each of them filled with their own thoughts. So strange was the setting, so peculiar a location, so unlikely that a tribe would live in such an alien place, that they were almost unable to believe what they were seeing.

Then, as though to tantalize them further, or perhaps to spare them from the unreality of the scene, a mist sprung up, seemingly out of nowhere, rising from the ground in streamers. Silently, before their disbelieving eyes, the village was swallowed up by the mists, vanishing as rapidly as it had appeared, as though it had never been.

They looked at each other with shocked eyes, wondering if they had imagined it, or if the village had been but a vision, some magical image fashioned by the Gods.

Fog began to blur their own images, settling in thicker and more dense than they had ever experienced. They were but a hand's breadth apart, but it soon became difficult to see one another.

Dawn gasped and, stifling a cry of fear, reached out with both hands and grasped Hawk and Emri firmly, as though by doing so she might anchor them and herself to the ground.

Then, softly, so softly as to play upon the ear like a dream that lingers on the edge of consciousness, they began to hear sounds, mere threads of tone, ghostly fragments that sounded like manifestations of the fog itself rather than actual sound. And yet it drew them on, hauntingly sweet, tantalizing and teasing in its quiet insistence.

So fragile was the sound, so intently did they listen, that they began to wonder if they had but imagined the ghostly sibilance through simple desire.

The fog swirled thick around them, cloaking their bodies and causing bits and pieces of them to vanish and then reappear. Mosca pressed hard against Emri's legs, all but invisible beneath the heaviest layer of mist, throwing Emri off-stride and causing him to stumble. Yet he did not complain, knowing that the cat was undoubtedly more afraid than they.

The sounds were all around them now, first on one side, then the next, ahead of them, then falling behind and disappearing. They stumbled toward the sounds using them like guideposts in the gloom, guideposts that vanished as they approached.

At first it seemed to be a hooting sound, like that of an owl, then it became more like that of a whistle, but muted and mellow and mysterious. One thing was clear: whatever it was, it was friendly, holding no malice whatsoever.

Emri, Hawk, and Dawn stumbled forward, trusting

the soft sounds. Mosca huddled at their feet, squalling his displeasure and hissing despite their words of reassurance.

The sound of the water, thick with ice as it sloshed against the shore, was loud in their ears, and the ground underfoot took on a different texture, softer, grainier, yet somehow stiff. And there was wind on their faces although the mist did not move.

The whistles—for that was what Emri had decided they were—lured them on, soft, haunting, hypnotic. And then, suddenly, there were hands on them, on their arms and shoulders, pulling them gently, guiding them, and once, just the tiniest hint of a giggle.

Emri allowed himself to be propelled wherever the hands led him. Strangely, he did not feel the slightest bit threatened, nor feel the need to raise spear or club. Even Mosca had stopped growling, and no longer pressed himself against Emri's legs.

The hands pressed against his arms gently, signaling him to stop, and then, although he heard no sound, no footsteps other than his own, no breath other than that of his companions, he knew that their mysterious guides had somehow withdrawn.

He began to wonder if they had somehow passed over into the world of the spirits, if any of it were real. He wondered, but he did not speak, for to have broken the silence would have violated the moment. Now only the whistles whispered their forlorn message into the cold, misty air.

Then, as though by magic, the mist began to lift, rolling round and round at first like water boiling, then drifting off in slow streamers stirred by a wind that was not felt. Bit by bit it floated away until only a light gauzy covering was left, and then, it too slowly dispersed.

As their eyes cleared, they found themselves standing on a beach made up of coarse granulated sand mixed with stones and ice crystals. The Endless Waters lay immediately to their left, rising and falling sluggishly, its surface completely clothed with ice.

The whistles still hooted and sounds of people could

now be heard. The village too was clearly seen, but none of that mattered. Standing in front of them, still wrapped in a mantle of clinging fog, was the figure of a man.

He stood quietly, saying nothing, scrutinizing them. He was small, smaller even than Dawn, although his back was humped and rounded with age and he leaned on a curved white stick, indicating that he might have been much taller in his youth.

On his head he wore the head of a great stag such as they had never seen. The skull fitted over the man's own mantle of white hair, the muzzle extending out over his forehead, the pelt draping down over his back. The weight of the skull with its great rack of spreading antlers must have been significant, but the old man gave no sign of discomfort.

His face was wrinkled and creased like a piece of ancient leather and had been burnished by the sun and wind of countless seasons. His eyes were rheumy and filmed with white, hooded by heavy lids that were drawn up at the outer edges. His nose was thin and beaked, like that of a hunting bird.

His small bent body, which gave no hint of fragility or weakness, was draped in the pelts of water beasts that crossed his chest and left his arms bare. Long, intricately carved bone ornaments dangled from his earlobes, and a broad necklet of bone and shell circled his neck. Black furskins draped the lower half of his body; and his feet and legs were wrapped in thick brown hide.

The silence stretched on as they examined each other. Even though Emri sensed the presence of many people behind him, it was a friendly silence that held no hint of danger.

"We have been waiting a long time for you to come," said the old man. The words were strange to the ear, twisted differently from the words that Tigers or even Toads spoke, but understandable, if one listened closely.

"We have been traveling for a long time," Emri replied, somehow not at all surprised to learn that they had been expected. "We have faced danger and suffered injury, but the ancestors guided our footsteps and now we are here. We offer you our respect and our talents, meager though they might be, and hope that you will not find us lacking."

"You speak well, cat man," said the old man. "The stones have told of your coming for a long time. They spoke of you and of one who visions and of the mother. You are our destiny and we are yours. We accept your respect and your talents, and if the stones speak true, we shall not find you lacking."

Having spoken these words, the old man seemed to falter, and from somewhere behind Emri, a younger man, though still old enough to be Emri's father, appeared and gently slipped his arm under that of the old man.

"We welcome you to our village," he said in a strong voice as he bowed low, head erect, meeting their gaze. His eyes were a rich brown, and shone with the importance of the moment. His hair and neck, ears and wrists were ornamented with shell and bone and the pelts of water beasts rode upon his back. But unlike the older man, he wore only a small loincloth and short boots upon his feet. He, like the older man, was several shades darker than they, and his eyes were also hooded and tilted up at the corners.

Emri returned the bow and Hawk and Dawn followed his lead. Mosca, untouched by the solemnity of the moment, yawned shrilly and, ambling forward, butted his head against the old man, demanding attention.

A titter of barely suppressed laughter swept through the unseen crowd and Emri felt his own lips twitch, even though horrified and completely surprised by Mosca's action.

The old man had nearly been knocked off his feet by Mosca's exuberant greeting. Steadied by the younger man's grip, he leaned over and stroked the cat between the eyes, speaking soft words that Emri could not hear. Whatever he said seemed to please the cat, for he sat down, leaned against the old man, and looked complacently at Emri.

Emri was astounded, for he would never have imagined that Mosca would desert him so readily and show such affection for a stranger. This, more than anything, more than the old man's words and talk of stones telling of their arrival, confused him, and brought a sense of unease into his heart.

"Do not worry," said the old man, his face crinkling into a mass of wrinkles as he smiled. "This one knows what is in my heart, and soon you will too. You are safe here with those who would be your friends."

Then, as though a signal had been given, they were surrounded by throngs of smiling people who told their names and laid soft hands on them in passing.

It was overwhelming. The names and faces blurred in their minds, only the common thread of brown skin, dark hooded eyes, and broad smiles linking them all together. Finally, the last of them had spoken and filed away, leaving only one person behind, a slender young woman dressed in brown deer furskins.

"I am Fawn Woman," she said in a soft voice, her eyes cast down on the beach shyly. "I will take you to your dwelling now." Making certain that they would follow, she turned and headed north along the strip of beach that led to the village.

Emri looked around in confusion, wondering where the old man had gone. He had not seen him leave, although he had tried to keep him in sight even when surrounded by the mass of people.

The crowd drifted ahead of them, casting quick glances at them from time to time when they thought they were not being observed, especially the children, who were far less subtle than their elders.

Fawn Woman led them to a curious round dwelling set amid others of identical construction and lifted a flap of skin that served as the doorway.

"Please enter," she said softly. "A fire has been laid for you and food is waiting. When you are rested, Father will speak with you."

She hovered for a moment, as though filled with uncertainty, and then said all in a rush, "I am glad you are here. He has been waiting for so long that I feared the stones had spoken wrong." Overcome by her own boldness, Fawn Woman's face flushed, and she dropped the flap as though it burned her fingers. Before they could speak, she was gone.

CHAPTER TWENTY-SEVEN

Emri, Dawn, and Hawk stood in the center of the dwelling and stared at each other, too confused and filled with conflicting emotions to speak.

Finally, Emri shrugged out of his heavy pack and lowered it to the ground. Hawk and Dawn followed his lead and then looked around them curiously.

It was a dwelling unlike any they had ever seen. The walls were formed by a circle of rib bones embedded butt first in the ground, the thinner ends rising in a gentle arch to meet at a point above their heads.

But such rib bones! Never before had they seen any so large. Surely these bones were bigger and longer than the largest of tuskers!

Heavy hides were stretched taut across the bone supports and fastened with stout thongs. The edges were weighted to the ground with large stones. A smoke hole was neatly cut in the center of the roof and ringed by the rib tips, which were neatly separated by smaller lengths of curved bone. It was such an ingenious arrangement that Emri found himself turning in circles admiring its unique construction, exclaiming over each new thing.

Dawn, ever more practical, was more concerned with their immediate needs. The center of the floor was taken up by a circular firepit, neatly ringed with smooth round stones. A low steady fire was burning in the pit, and stacked to one side was a small pile of bones and dried dung cakes. Large flat vertebrae were set on either side of the fire pit, easily able to seat a man comfortably.

"Look," Dawn cried excitedly, and as the men

turned to her, she showed them a tripod made of smaller ribs that could be set in holes on three sides of the fire. Once in place, the tripod was the perfect height for cooking above the fire.

Dawn rifled through her pack, looking for her cooking pouch and something to cook, anxious to try out the ingenious arrangement. She had withdrawn a handful of smoked deer meat when there was a subtle scratch on the door flap and, after a brief hesitation, it was pulled aside.

Three women entered the dwelling, Fawn Woman and two others, older and heavier-set. Fawn Woman smiled at them shyly with downcast eyes and then said in a voice barely above that of a whisper, "My father sends you food and hopes that it is to your liking."

Dawn hastened to reply. As she sought to reassure the young woman, who was only slightly younger than she herself, Mosca—who had been eyeing the hunk of smoked meat—leaped forward, snatched it from her hands, and disappeared through the loose flap. There was a heartbeat of startled silence and then everyone began to laugh.

"That one!" fussed Dawn, laughing still, "he is like a small child. You must beware of him, for he will take food whenever he can, and whatever else interests him if he is able!"

"I have a child like that," said one of the women, her dark eyes twinkling merrily, "but he does not have the excuse of being a cat!"

Everyone laughed again and the tension caused by newness was broken. Suddenly, there seemed much to speak of and everyone began to talk at once.

Amid much laughter, the women placed the food they had brought on the ground in front of the fire. Then, reaching over to the edges of the dwelling, they pulled hides out of the shadows, hides that had been fashioned into large pouches and stuffed with sedge and grass. These, too, could be used as cushions for seating and also for sleeping, explained the heavier of the two women, whose name was Whistling Bird. To demonstrate her name, she uttered a soft sad cry, that of a bird who nested in the sedges and hunted the cold waters. The sound was remarkably accurate and they applauded her, which brought a flush of pleasure to her round cheeks.

The women had brought stone platters mounded with baked fish, roasted birds, smoked deer meat, and a pouch filled with tender greens of a sort that was unfamiliar to them. There was also a large bowl carved out of stone that was filled with a fragrant steaming brew.

The smoke hole admitted a certain amount of light into the dwelling, as did the door flap which was made to be pinned back, but Fawn Woman also produced two long slender bowls that had been fashioned out of stone. These bowls were filled to the brim with a clear oily substance, and twisted moss wicks floated on their surface. Fawn Woman explained that they were to be used at night or whenever the weather forbade opening the flap; these were carefully set aside where they would not be overturned.

Although they were urged to stay, the women reluctantly took their leave, leaving their guests with more food than even Mosca could eat.

Their bellies stretched taut with more food than they had eaten in a long time, their senses soothed by the hot drink that tasted slightly tart yet pleasantly refreshing, Emri, Dawn, and Hawk lay back on the soft cushions and talked, not even stirring when Mosca crept back into the dwelling and helped himself to the remains of the feast.

"What do you think the old man meant when he said he had been waiting for us?" Hawk asked voicing the thought that was foremost in their minds as he watched the play of firelight on the roof of the dwelling.

"I don't know," replied Emri. "Maybe he is their shaman. Perhaps he has had a vision that told him of our coming. Or perhaps they have been watching us and waiting for us to arrive."

"I don't care how they knew about us," said Dawn. "I like them and they seem to like us. We can make our home with them and be safe."

"But what about the followers?" asked Hawk. "Do

you think that they have turned back? What if they are still tracking us? What if they find us? Killing a totem is a terrible thing. Maybe they will tell these people what we have done and they will cast us out!"

"There is no way of knowing," said Emri after a time of thought. "No good will come of worrying about a thing that may not happen. Perhaps the followers were not so lucky as we and drowned in the crossing. Or maybe they survived the water and were killed by the bears. Many things might have happened. We may never know the end of it."

"But, Emri . . ." cried Hawk.

"We will tell our story to the Old One," said Emri, holding up his hand to halt Hawk's words. "If he does not understand, we will leave and find another clan, but somehow I do not think that the Old One will be troubled. Surely he has seen much in his long years. There is wisdom in the lines of his face."

"Truly it is so," said Hawk, mulling over what Emri had said.

"This is our home, now. We are not leaving," Dawn said softly, her arms clasped around her knees as she stared dreamily into the fire. Turning to look at Emri, the firelight still dancing in her eyes, she said, "We are home now," with a sense of finality that put an end to the conversation.

Lost in their own thoughts, comforted by the warmth of the fire and their own full bellies, they slipped off into sleep, one after the other.

Later, Emri was wakened by a soft sound, like that of a rodent gnawing on a bone. He opened his eyes and smiled to see the play of firelight on the darkened dome. The glitter of stars told him that it was night.

The sound came again and he stirred, evoking a sleeply grumble from Mosca, who was curled against his side. Slipping out from under the weight of the cat and moving softly so as not to waken Dawn and Hawk, he lifted the doorflap and looked outside.

"My father would like you to join him at his fire," Fawn Woman said softly, barely visible in the dark shadows.

"We would be honored," said Emri, and lowering the doorflap, he shook Dawn and Hawk into wakefulness and told them of the summons.

They straightened their garments and smoothed their hair and discussed the possibilities of leaving Mosca behind, for they did not know what to expect from the cat among large numbers of people. It was decided that he would probably cause more mischief if he were excluded than if he were brought along, and so he accompanied them as they left the dwelling.

A sharp breeze struck them like a blow as they left the shelter, whistling down from the north and sweeping across the icy water. They clutched their garments to them and hurried across the icy sand, following Fawn Woman's shadowy form.

The Old One's dwelling was identical to their own, only slightly larger. Fawn Woman lifted the doorflap and gestured for them to enter.

A large fire lit up the interior of the dwelling, heating the air so that it felt like a day in Warm Time. The Old One sat close to the fire, the immense stag skull on his head, his robes wrapped about him though Emri could already feel moisture sprouting on his own forehead.

The younger man sat beside the Old One and his eyes held the look of one who dreads what is to come. Emri stared at him intently, wondering what the man feared and how it might affect them.

The old man gestured with his hand, motioning them to a place in front of him that had been spread with cushions and furskins. As they took their places, Emri noted that the walls were lined with seated figures, tribal elders, men who were wrinkled and bent with age, all of whom watched them with patient eyes. Fawn Woman bowed low to her father and, without glancing at them again, slipped from the dwelling.

Without speaking, the Old One dipped his hand into a stone bow and sprinkled a coarse white powder on the fire. Instantly, the air was filled with the heady redolence of pine sap, the scent so intense that Emri felt his head spin.

The Old One dipped his hand a second time and a mist seemed to form and hang on the air. The firelight flickered through the mist, casting strange shadows against the walls of the dwelling. Emri became conscious of a low throbbing, and for a short time, he wondered if it was the blood beating in his ears. Then he realized that it was a drum, pulsing low and constant, almost below the level of awareness.

Dawn swayed and Emri put out a hand to steady her as a gourd rattle began a whispery *chink, chink, chink*. And somewhere in the background was the haunting cry of the whistle.

"We are the People," intoned the Old One, his voice husky and disembodied. "We are the People of the Deer. We have followed the deer long moons out of memory through sun and rain and snow. Their path has been our path; their life, our life; their death, our death."

The scent of pines seemed to grow more intense though the Old One's hands had not moved. As Emri listened, forms seemed to take shape in the mist.

Emri felt a bolt of fire drill through his body as he looked into the liquid eyes of a stag so close that he could smell the rank pungency of a male in rut. The stag's nose twitched once as it probed the mist for signs of danger. Its big ears flickered and then, dipping its rack of horns, it vanished into the mist from which it had appeared. A sharp gasp from Hawk told Emri that he was not alone in viewing the misty apparition.

"We are the People of the Deer," said the Old One, continuing as though nothing odd had occurred. "We were many. We were strong. Our enemies ran before us, for our spears were sharp and our aim was true. We had many sons and our daughters were lovely to look on. There was laughter and happiness in our dwellings.

"We are the People of the Deer, and where the deer lead we must follow, for they are the way and the life.

"We are the People of the Deer. When they feed, we are fed. When they multiply, we are many, we are strong. When they go hungry and their numbers diminish, so must we decline.

"We are the People of the Deer, and when they ar
gone, so must we vanish from the earth. We are th
People of the Deer."

For a time there was only the sound of the rattle
the drum, the whistle, and the wail of old voices.

The Old One's words had entered Emri's mind an
still echoed in his head. He tried to focus on what ha
been said. Something, something was wrong. He looke
to Hawk, but Hawk was breathing heavily, his chi
resting on his chest, and Dawn lay limp against Emri
shoulder. Even Mosca was staring into the fire, mout
open, panting, his eyes glazed. Nor did he stir whe
Emri reached out and touched him.

Emri shook his head to clear it from the cloyin
scent and felt himself reel. As he put out a hand to stead
himself, he saw the deer again, running swift and free
passing through the walls in front of him as though the
did not exist.

Wave after wave of deer poured through the hid
walls; great stags with towering racks; yearling buck:
proud and confident, their powerful haunches ripplin
with muscle; shy does with young ones trotting at the
sides; and newborn fawns with huge ears and shinin
eyes.

So real were they, so real the smell of grassy dung an
earth and sun-warmed pelts, that Emri twisted to on
side to avoid the sharp hooves that trod the air beside h
head. And then, suddenly, they were no more. Em
looked around him in amazement to see where the
could have gone.

"They are gone," said the old one, in a voice r
longer strong. "The deer are gone. But the peop
remain and soon we too will vanish."

Emri felt the words rise up upon his lips and th
need to speak was heavy. "We have seen the deer; the
are not gone," he blurted out, but it was as though h
had not spoken.

"The stones have told of one who will come
intoned the old man. "He who will lead us back to th
deer. He who will give us new life. He is to come with
cat at his side. He is the one.

"The stones have told of one who will come with the spirit and the head of a hawk; this one will speak to the ancestors and guide us to the Gods.

"The stones have spoken of one who will come who will be the mother of us all, she who is to give us new life. The stones have spoken and it is true."

The Old One's voice dwindled away to a thready whisper and then was silent. The rattles stopped, fading slowly away to a sigh, then the drums, and, last of all, the melancholy whistles.

Emri sat still upon the blanket of skins, unable to move, his mind still filled with the vision of what he had seen. But what had he seen? Surely a herd of deer had not passed through the dwelling walking on the air! But remembering them as they had looked, the smell of them still lingering in his nostrils, he could not convince himself otherwise.

"The stones have spoken," the Old One said at last. "We have prayed. We have believed. We have waited, and now you are here. Will you stay with us and learn? And when the time comes, will you fulfill the prophecy of the stones?"

Dawn lifted her head from Emri's shoulder and pushed her hair back from her face. Hawk straightened his shoulders and glanced at Emri. Together, they faced the old man across the fire and nodded in solemn agreement.

CHAPTER TWENTY-EIGHT

Broken Tooth and Walks Alone followed the trail as far as they were able, then lost it finally in a maze of deeply cut deer tracks.

Broken Tooth sighed with relief when even Walks Alone was forced to admit after two days of cold driving rain that the trail would not be found again.

He packed his pouch on the morning of the third day, his heart sitting light in his chest, and turned his face toward home. Not even the thought of the fearsome voyage by floater that lay ahead was enough to quell his good spirits. Thus, it came as a great shock when Walks Alone set off in the opposite direction, still heading north.

"Where are you going?" he cried aloud in dismay. "They are gone! The trail has vanished! We will never find them. Give up and let us return to our women and our fires!"

Walks Alone, who had no woman to sit beside him at the fire, did not deign to answer but continued walking.

"Stop!" cried Broken Tooth, running alongside Walks Alone and grabbing hold of his arm. "It is enough! They have won!"

Walks Alone stopped abruptly and flung Broken Tooth's hand off his arm. "You do not tell me when to stop," he said harshly. "You, you are nothing! You cannot tell me what should be done. Leave! Quit! Go home to your woman and your fire. I will go on alone!"

"But where! Where will you go?" pleaded Broken

Tooth, hoping to waken Walks Alone to the impossibility of the task. "There is no trail."

"I need no trail," said Walks Alone, the anger fading from his eyes, and speaking as much to himself as to the other man.

"There is nowhere left for them to go but forward," he said softly as he gazed ahead, unseeing. "They cannot go to the east, for there is no passage, only mountains of ice. They cannot go west, for there is only water. The only way they can go is forward. I will follow and I will find them. And when I do, I will kill them."

Broken Tooth stood and watched him go, struggling with his indecision. He did not want to go on, not one step further. But neither did he want to return by himself. The long journey was far too dangerous for a man alone. He would do best to follow Walks Alone until even he was forced to admit that the quest was over. Shouldering his pack, worry sitting heavy on his heart, he followed in the other's footsteps.

CHAPTER TWENTY-NINE

The learning, as the Old One had put it, began on the morning of the following day. Fawn Woman scratched upon the doorflap shortly after dawn and greeted them in the same shy manner they had come to expect.

Emri was taken to the Old One, whose name was Taug, while Hawk was greeted by the younger man who had stood at Taug's arm. His name was Speaker to the Deer and he was the shaman of the clan. Dawn took her place among the women, who welcomed her with the outstretched arms of old familiar friends. Mosca divided his time among them all.

As Leaf Fall dwindled into Cold Time, they developed a pattern that governed their days. From dawn until dusk they sat at the sides of their respective teachers. The nights were theirs.

Some days, Taug would speak to Emri, repeating from memory the long history of the People of the Deer. Names of those long gone to the campfires in the sky were recalled, as well as the deeds they had performed while on earth—some glorious, and some as black as the heart of a thieving weasel.

Other days Taug would be sunk within himself, his filmed eyes gazing inward where none could share the vision or the pain, his spirit wandering in the shadows of the past or the mists of the future, and he spoke no words at all. At these times, Emri learned to sit in silence, waiting for Taug's spirit to return to his body, giving what comfort and support he was able through his presence.

He learned through tales what was expected of one who would lead a people, what others had done before him, and the wisdom or the folly of their actions.

Time after time, Taug would tell him of incidents that had beset the clan at some point in their long history. The people who lived those times had become real to Emri, so real that he could call their images to mind with the mere mention of their names.

Once the story was told, Taug would ask Emri what he would have done. Only when Emri answered did Taug tell him the end of the story, revealing the outcome of that ancient chief's decision. In time, Emri was pleased to note that his answers were seldom wrong and that he had avoided several serious mistakes that other chiefs had made. But on a day that he was feeling quite good about himself, he managed to lose an entire party of hunters beneath the feet of a herd of wooly tuskers. Fortunately, the chief whose decision it had been originally, had not made the same mistake. He had successfully driven a tusker over the edge of a cliff where it had fallen to its death, providing food for the clan for several moons. In this way Emri gained wisdom tempered with humility.

Emri learned from Taug and Speaker that hairy tuskers, along with deer, had once been plentiful along the coast. Now they appeared but seldom. And—while their infrequent arrival brought joy to the camp, signalling the opportunity for fresh meat—the tuskers also brought danger and death if their presence was not noted well in advance.

Hawk and Speaker had become close friends, sometimes communicating without the need for words. Hawk's ability to vision animals in stone and line was developed greatly under Speaker's tutelage, for the man had similar talents of his own.

Colors were impossible to come by, for there was no earth other than sand and gray clay mixed with ground rock and shells. But there was charcoal and stones, tusks and bones to carve on.

Hawk also learned to make the whistles. They were

made from the leg bones of birds and deer and were used for everything from signals to ceremonies.

Speaker also taught Hawk about drumming. First he learned to beat a simple cadence, then he learned to hold it. Drummings were used to draw the attention of the Gods to those who needed their help. Drummings for simple ceremonies were short and required little effort. But healings and more significant occasions required great stamina and the ability to lose oneself in the rhythm.

At first Hawk had difficulty in drumming for long periods of time; his arms grew tired and his head ached. But then, under Speaker's tutelage he learned to open himself to the rhythm and become one with the sound. At such times, it seemed that his physical body disappeared, vanished, crumbled away like a heavy shell that was no longer needed, leaving his spirit shining brightly in its place.

As Leaf Fall passed into the early stages of Cold Time and the ice locked itself in solid ridges against the shore, Hawk was allowed to trance for the first time.

Guided by Speaker he journeyed to the past on the wings of a snow-white hawk. He viewed the vast herds of deer and the men who followed them. He saw the great wooly tuskers and the massive bison who darkened the earth with their numbers.

He soared above the earth as the tuskers and the bison, the deer and the antelope, the long necked camels and the tiny horses, and, last of all, the men who followed them, crossed from one world to the next.

He was there when the Cold Time grew longer, longer than ever before, covering the land with ice and snow and creeping forward relentlessly till the world was white as far as the eye could see.

Dawn learned no less than the men. She had learned well at her mother's knee, absorbing all that her clan had to offer in the gathering of foodstuffs, healing, preparation of meat, the working of hides, and how to live off the land.

But more was required of her here in this harsh land. Long she listened to Washona, the ancient crone

who was the first wife of Taug, and she learned much
about healing that she had not known.

She also learned the names of the campfires in the
skies and how to find her way from one to the other
should she become lost. And she learned how to survive
in a land that was seldom green.

Mosca alone was free to roam, and this he did,
adding a thick layer of fat beneath the heavy pelt.
Although cold enough to freeze water, the air was dry
and felt no worse than the bitter wet cold of the southern
peaks where Emri, Hawk, and Mosca had spent the
previous Cold Time.

Of more concern to them than the cold was the
constant-threatening menace of the mountain of ice that
hung over the village, terrifying by its presence alone.

Emri caught himself glancing up at the blue-white
mountain countless times a day and never did he grow
accustomed to it. Always, it took his breath away by its
sheer imposing bulk.

Hawk was curiously impassive on the subject and
would not speak of it at all. Dawn was completely and
totally terrified by its threat.

Several days after they arrived, a woman was killed
as she drew water from the face of the mountain at one of
the many seeps. An overhang broke off without warning
and fell, crushing her beneath its mass.

But this was not the worst of it. South of the village,
at the base of the lobe of ice that reached out toward the
water, there was what appeared to be the mouth of a
cave.

The ice was pure white in color, but the mouth of
the cave glistened pale blue and grew increasingly
darker the deeper one went.

Improbable as it seemed, people did venture inside
the cave, for it was believed that this cave was a source of
great power—a tunnel that led from the land of the
living to the world of the spirits. Only by venturing far
into the dark icy cavern, it was believed, could one truly
speak to the Gods. The likelihood that the Gods would
hear one was in direct proportion to how far one
traveled.

Neither Emri nor Hawk liked this practice, yet

found difficulty in avoiding it when Taug or Speaker required their presence. Dawn went once and thereafter refused to step foot inside the cave again, despite Washona's obvious disapproval.

Mosca was the object of much attention, popular with the children, who sought his favor by saving tasty bits of their food. The cat's appetite was voracious, in keeping with his steady growth, and he was all too willing to take whatever they gave him. He rewarded their efforts by playing with them, running beside them on the hard-packed snow as they shrilled happily, chasing bits of bone that he generally ate.

The adults seemed to accept Emri, Hawk, and Dawn as wholeheartedly as the children did Mosca. So far as any of them could tell, there was no resentment or hostility anywhere, despite the fact that they, three total strangers from outside the clan, were being groomed for positions of power. Not understanding how this could be, Hawk asked Speaker about it one afternoon as the flaming sun set slowly above the frozen waters, its glowing rays spreading across the snow and ice like a sheet of fire.

"The stones have told of your coming for so long that we have always known it would happen," replied Speaker, avoiding Hawk's eyes and staring out across the frozen expanse. "There is no point in arguing with destiny. What must be, must be."

Once again Hawk felt the same sense of dread that he had first noted in Speaker. Yet he said nothing, knowing that it was Speaker's place to say what was on his mind. For Hawk to have asked would have been a rudeness and an invasion of the other man's personal thoughts.

To break the awkward moment Hawk asked, "Tell me more about the stones, for I do not truly understand how they are used."

Speaker, relieved to have the subject changed, reached for the small leather pouch that hung from a thong around his neck. Opening the mouth of the pouch, he shook a handful of pebbles into his hand and held them out to Hawk.

They slid into Hawk's hand and he turned them over one at a time, examining them carefully. Finally, he lifted confused eyes to Speaker. "I do not understand," he said. "These look like plain, ordinary rocks to me. I do not see anything special about them. How is it that they can tell you anything, much less things of great importance?"

"Things are not always what they seem," Speaker said, a small smile lifting the corners of his mouth. "Even the most simple things are sometimes more complicated than they would seem at first glance.

"You must look closely," he said, picking up first one stone then another. "Here," he said, pointing to a smooth brown stone that had several lines running through it. "This is the sign of the land, and here, this white stone with the two branching points is the sign for deer. This stone bears the impression of a man, and this one a river. Each of them bears the sign of something: man, woman, child, animals, trees, rivers, snow, ice, things that surround us.

"These," he said, pulling a second pouch from beneath his tunic top, "are the helpers." He poured a smaller handful of oddly-shaped items out into the palm of his hand for Hawk to examine.

There were short sticks and long ones, a spearpoint, circles of shell, bits of moss, a tree leaf, pine needles, a small antler, pieces of fur from a variety of animals, a smooth black stone, bark from a tree, a dried beetle, and many other oddments.

"I still do not understand how it works," said Hawk. "Is it not the same, always?"

"No," said Speaker. "I will show you how it is done. First you draw a circle on the ground." And sweeping the ground in front of the fire smooth and free of stones, he drew a circle with the end of his finger.

"Now you must ask a question," said Speaker.

"What kind of question?" asked Hawk.

"Anything," Speaker said with a shrug. "Whatever you would like to know."

Many things ran through Hawk's mind—Would Dawn ever love him? Would she ever be his woman? Would they ever return to their own lands?—but he was afraid to ask for fear of learning the answer. Instead, he said, "What lies in the immediate future?" thinking it a safe question that would result in nothing more than news of a hunt that was to take place the next day.

Speaker poured the stones back inside the leather pouch, shook them up, then tossed the sack up, while holding it at the bottom. There was a shower of stones and a number of them fell inside the circle while others fell outside the lines.

Hawk watched intently as Speaker did the same with the contents of the second bag. But he did not even glance at the inner circle until all of those things that had fallen outside the lines had been returned to their respective bags.

"Now we begin," he said, and he leaned forward and studied the circle and all it contained. Suddenly, his body grew still and he turned to Hawk and looked at him searchingly.

"What—what is it?" asked Hawk, his mouth suddenly dry, wondering what Speaker had seen. He leaned forward and stared at the stones himself, although he could make no sense of what he saw.

"Two men," said Speaker, after a long moment's hesitation. "Two men will arrive from the south. You see here: two stones, both men, here in the bottom of the circle. Here in the center, this stone is the village. One of the men has a short leg or has suffered a leg injury," he said, holding up each stone as he spoke of it so that Hawk might see and understand.

"They do not come with peace in their hearts," he said, holding up the spearpoint. "They come for blood. They come for you." And he slowly picked up the last three items in the circle, a black stone streaked with white in the shape of a hawk, a stone with the crude outline of a stick man and a cat found in its creases, and a round reddish-gold stone that bulged on its lower half like the belly of a pregnant woman.

Hawk tried to laugh, to make a joke that would

relieve the tension, but it was as though he had swallowed a stone and no sound emerged.

Speaker quickly scooped the stones back into their bags and drew them shut, as though that might undo what had been told.

Finally, in an unusual gesture, he placed his hand on Hawk's thin shoulder and squeezed gently.

"We are your people now. No harm will come to you in our camp. Of that you may be sure."

"Did you see that in the stones?" Hawk asked hoarsely. "Did they say that all would be well?" But though Speaker squeezed his arm yet again, he did not answer.

CHAPTER THIRTY

Even though they had been expecting them, it was still a shock to see the figures of the two men appear on the crest of the ice lobe. The story had spread quickly, and now the entire village stood in silence watching the men approach.

There was a moment of hesitation, a time of indecision, as the two men realized that they were being observed. Hawk prayed to the spirits in that small heartbeat, that the men would turn back in the face of so many. But his hopes were ill-founded, for the men straightened their shoulders and came on with bold steps and spears held at the ready.

They advanced to well within spear range, as though to show that they had no fear, before they came to a final halt. A strange silence fell between the two groups.

The People of the Deer remained silent, for it was Emri's place to speak to the men who were from his own tribe. For them to have spoken before Emri would have decreased his standing within their tribe, seeming as though he were hiding behind them.

"Ho, brothers. I see you, Walks Alone. I see you, Broken Tooth," Emri said in neutral tones, hoping that his voice sounded strong and unafraid, although his heart had plummeted when he recognized Walks Alone.

"Ho!" replied Walks Alone, his upper lip curling in a cold sneer. "I see you too, but you are no brother of mine—only a brother to the weasel."

All around Emri there were muted gasps and low murmurings as the People of the Deer took in the terrible insult. Emri felt their eyes on his back as they waited to see how he would react.

"We welcome you to our village, brothers," said Emri, ignoring the harsh words. "Your journey has been long and hard. Let us offer you warmth and shelter, and hot food and drink for your bellies."

"We do not want your hospitality," said Walks Alone. "The only thing we want, we will take . . . your lives." He made as though to raise his spear.

"Stop!" We should not lift our hands against each other," cried Dawn as she ran halfway between the two groups and looked from one to the other in desperation. "We are clan. Let us talk and try to settle our differences before we turn to violence."

Walks Alone's face was hard and unyielding.

"Come inside," begged Dawn, her eyes fastened on Broken Tooth, who was the eldest child of her mother's sister and had always been fond of her. "It is not proper that important matters be discussed while standing outside in the ice and snow. Come inside."

"It could not hurt," Broken Tooth said hesitantly, raising his eyes to Walks Alone's face. "Let us take shelter. I am cold and my belly is empty."

"You are an old woman," snarled Walks Alone. "We have come to kill, not to fill our bellies."

Then, something strange and almost unbelievable happened. As Walks Alone turned back toward Emri, Fawn Woman—shy, unobtrusive Fawn Woman—stepped forward and slowly crossed the distance between the two parties. Ignoring the long, deadly spear, she stood directly in front of Walks Alone and studied his face intently almost as though she had never seen a man before.

A murmuring ripple passed through the crowd as they gazed at the young woman who could scarcely speak to those she had known all her life without blushing and stammering in shyness. There were those who were also concerned that this strange action might cause some violent reaction from the bloodthirsty stranger. This was not to be, for Walks Alone had lowered his

spear and was now staring into the eyes of Fawn Woman
with the same disbelieving rapt expression.

Suddenly, it was as though they were the only two
people left in the world, certainly the only two people
left on the snow-swept beach. Tension drained from the
air as people let out their breath and looked at one
another, searching for an explanation. Feet scuffled and a
child giggled before he was roughly shaken by his
mother.

Ignoring everything but the man in front of her,
Fawn Woman reached out and laid a small gentle hand
on the side of his face, and after a moment, he covered it
with his own. They continued looking at each other
without movement until the others around them grew
restless. Broken Tooth in particular seemed most confused as to what was happening.

Dawn, seizing the opportunity to further neutralize
the situation, touched Broken Tooth on the arm.
"Please, brother, let us offer you the warmth of our fire;
you are cold and your belly is empty."

Broken Tooth hesitated, looking over at Walks
Alone for denial or acquiescence, but Walks Alone made
no movement or gesture at all. Broken Tooth took a few
uncertain steps that grew more buoyant the further the
distance grew between them.

A large number of the curious villagers followed
them as they made their way to Emri's dwelling. As
many as could fit, including Taug and Speaker, crowded
inside to hear what would be said. The remainder stayed
on the beach watching the motionless Fawn Woman and
Walks Alone.

There had not been so much of interest happening
in the village since the time four Warm Times previous
when a family of six of the enormous gray fish had swum
straight up onto the beach, sacrificing themselves to the
People of the Deer.

Inside Emri's dwelling, Broken Tooth looked
around him with open admiration and smiled uncertain-
ly at the broad impassive faces that stared at him from all
sides. At his smile, their stolid expressions fell aside and

they smiled in return, their wide brown faces crinkling
in happiness that the day was not to end in bloodshed.

Some of the women slipped out of the dwelling,
rushing off to bring back a contribution of food to the
feast that was surely to come, hurrying so as not to miss
the storytelling.

Others, those who had been unable to squeeze into
the dwelling, slipped inside, taking the places of those
who left. The remainder huddled outside the open
doorflap where they would at least be able to hear what
was being said.

Throughout the long day and well into the night,
Broken Tooth regaled his spellbound audience with the
tale of their journey. The People of the Deer gasped and
shrieked and covered their eyes, but never their ears,
and begged for repetitions of the more exciting bits.

Emri, Dawn, and Hawk were also forced to tell
their own story once again, even though it had been told
many, many times before. The two stories were com-
pared and fitted together like parts of a puzzle.

Then, Emri and Hawk were made to tell their story
from the very beginning, when they had first met and
killed Mosca's mother, forging their friendship through
pain and adversity.

The dwelling was sweltering with the heat of many
bodies packed close together when the storytelling was
finally done, and the stars were growing dim in the pale
sky.

New arrivals had told them when Fawn Woman and
Walks Alone left the open beach and sought the warmth
and privacy of her shelter, closing out those who
attempted to follow.

There had been no sign of them since. Those who
were of Fawn Woman's family and shared her dwelling
made other arrangements amid much comic sighing,
giggling, and even a few good-natured, but crude, finger
mimes.

The morning broke fair and cold, the pale watery
sun streaming over the frigid landscape, trickling down
through the smoke holes of the dwellings and calling to
the People of the Deer.

They responded groggily, staggering outside and

urinating in the snow, feeling their heads throb from the excesses of the previous night.

They peered painfully upward, then blinked and turned aside. The sun was too bright and their bodies too slow for hunting. That decision made, they hurried back to Emri's dwelling, bearing smoked fish and fowl, just in case the stranger happened to be awake and in the mood for talk.

Walks Alone and Fawn Woman were not seen for four days and nights, emerging, if at all, only when curious, but friendly, eyes were asleep. The village buzzed with talk.

On the morning of the fifth day, they came out of the dwelling, bringing all activity to a halt and drawing the villagers to them by the sheer force of their presence alone.

They were changed, different. That was readily apparent. Fawn Woman no longer looked at the ground, her eyes downcast and blushing frequently. This Fawn Woman looked at all who gathered with a proud eye and head held high, her chin pointed toward those who waited to see what new exciting development would occur.

Walks Alone was equally changed. He stood beside Fawn Woman, hands resting easily at his sides, the grim, harsh look absent from his face, his dark eyes calm and at peace.

It was clear that each had recognized something in the other and, in the days and nights of their confinement, had forged a bond that strengthened them separately and together made them whole.

Fawn Woman took Walks Alone to her father, and before the moon man filled his hollow belly, the rites were performed that joined them together forever.

Emri, Hawk, and Dawn were present at the rites, as were all other members of the village, and at the feast that followed.

The four of them came face to face at one point of the celebration, and Walks Alone was the first to drop his eyes and turn away, confusion taking the place of the fury and hatred that had driven the man for all his long, and lonely life.

In the long days of Cold Time that were to follow, as the Wind Gods breathed their icy breath on the land and life grew harsh, Walks Alone proved himself the best hunter among them. He crouched for long hours, motionless beside the air hole of the great black sea beasts, spearing them as they leaped out of the water and slithered onto the ice. He speared fish through holes in the ice and snared birds as they came to rest.

Once, while prowling the lonely stretches of broken ice that piled against the shore, he encountered an immense white bear, a male, huge and deadly with long sharp fangs and terrible claws. He slew the beast alone, with only one long claw mark across his face, to tell of the difficult victory.

He bore the kill home to the village and presented it to Fawn Woman in front of all. She shared out the meat, but kept the beautiful furskin for her own as a sign of her man's prowess and caring.

Not even Emri could fear Walks Alone any longer, so great was his transformation and his joyful pride when Fawn Woman became great with child. Looking on him, his harsh face softened, laugh lines appearing at the corners of his eyes, it was hard to remember the terrible person he had once been.

During these long happy days and nights, the only hint of a problem came from the mountain of ice that hung above them like the shadow of a great carrion-eating bird of death.

Always frightening, the mountain had begun to make noises and sounds that struck fear into Emri's heart and caused Dawn to draw the furskins over her head at night and cower in the darkness.

"I am afraid, Emri," she cried one night as the mountain groaned and creaked like some living thing in pain. "I am afraid that it will fall and kill us all. "Let us leave this place, let us take the people and go somewhere better. It is too cold here, and I miss trees and rivers and green things. I want to be warm again, and raise our child in a land that is kinder than this one."

Emri stared at her in surprise. She smiled back tremulously, tears streaking her cheeks, confirming the fact that she was to have another child again, at last.

Hawk turned aside, unhappiness lying heavy on his heart, and he knew that Dawn would never be his. Then he heard Speaker's words echoing in his head, saying, "It does no good to argue with destiny. What will be, will be," and he knew that it was true.

"We will go," promised Emri, holding Dawn close to him. "But I must find the right moment to speak to Taug. He is old and has spent his life in this place. He will not leave it easily."

"But, Emri, the stones have told of our coming and have said that we would lead the people to find the deer," sniffed Dawn, wiping her cheeks with her fingers. "Why would Taug not want to leave? We are fulfilling his own prophecy."

"Saying something and doing it are not always the same," replied Emri. "We will leave—this I promise— but it must be done rightly, with Taug's approval. He has been good to us and I would not cause him hurt. I will look for a sign that may be used to argue in our favor."

"Do not be long, Emri," begged Dawn. "Do not be long."

CHAPTER THIRTY-ONE

Cold Time wrapped its cruel hands around the People of the Deer and squeezed. The sun rose late and set early and there was no warmth in its rays. Snow had fallen heavier and harder than usual, and storms aimed themselves at the small village and pounded them with savage fury.

On the few rare days that the storms were absent, the men hurried out of their dwellings and searched land and ice for game. But the game had seemingly fled the land, and hunger was added to cold.

Fuel was also in short supply, for there had been no sign of deer or tuskers and all dung that existed had long since been gathered. Fires burned low as families merged into larger units in an effort to warm themselves with shared hardships as well as body heat.

Taug decreed that the gods must be importuned on behalf of the people, and everyone was urged to go into the cave of ice and speak into the ear of the Gods.

Much as Emri did not wish to do so, there was no way that he could avoid accompanying Taug on such a mission. Hawk was required to go as well, walking behind Speaker and drumming a rhythm meant to draw the God's attention.

As the long line of people entered the cold blue cavern, it seemed to Emri that something had changed. The flow of milky white water that always ran along the smoothly scoured floor had frozen with the intense cold. But even that was not the difference.

It seemed to Emri as though the Gods were holding their breath. There was a palpable sense of anticipation,

of a waiting for something to happen hanging in the
frigid air of the tunnel.

If anyone else noticed the difference, they did not
say, but merely hurried through the cold tunnel, mur-
mured their prayers, and left as quickly as was considered proper.

Emri and Hawk did not escape so easily, for Taug
and Speaker followed the tortuous path of the tunnel
into the cold heart of the mountain.

The walls closed in around them, the shadows thick
and black behind them, the darkness barely illuminated
by the weak flickering of the oil lamps. The curved walls
were similar in appearance to the gullet of a bird, smooth
arches intersected by rings, and it was hard to avoid the
feeling of being swallowed whole by some gigantic
animal.

Emri was glad beyond words when they reached
the end of the tunnel, a place where the path was
intersected by a deep crevasse that seemed to reach into
the very depths of the earth. The bottom could not be
seen. It was here that Taug and Speaker said their
prayers, hoping that they would reach the ears of the
Gods, and then made their way back to the village
followed by Emri, Hawk and those who counted themselves among the most faithful.

Fawn Woman was among these few, accompanied
by a reluctant Walks Alone, although Emri could see the
barely suppressed fear that lurked behind his dark eyes.
This common bond was the first link between the two
dissimilar men.

But in spite of their impassioned prayers, two small
bodies as well as four old ones joined the ancestors
before Cold Time began to relinquish its cruel grip. The
sun was the first sign of a returning life: rising sooner,
setting later, and shedding the tiniest hint of warmth at
peak of day.

The storms abated and the men ventured once
more out upon the ice, and succeeded in spearing three
large water beasts whose flesh was thickly layered with
life-giving fat.

The women wailed and wept for joy as the men slid

the carcasses back to the village and quickly cut the meat into large chunks that were shared out to each and every family. Few were able to resist the temptation to gobble the meat raw, and their bellies ached that night from the unaccustomed richness.

Mosca had suffered greatly during the Cold Time, and his bones protruded beneath his pelt like those of a living skeleton. It hurt them all to see him so and hear his unhappy moaning, but there was little to be done for him while others, less strong, were dying. With the luck of the kill, he was given bones, skin and all the parts that could be spared, and even Walks Alone made a silent secret contribution, taken from his own share.

Fawn Woman and Dawn had become gaunt during the long winter, and their bellies were small and hard instead of plump and full. This more than anything drove their men out onto the ice, longer than was perhaps wise, in search of game.

The days were becoming longer and warmer as well, and the ice was becoming unstable. More and more, they noticed cracks appearing in the ice, exposing the black water that lay beneath and causing the footing to be more treacherous.

Just as Walks Alone had been a fierce enemy, he had become an equally staunch friend, accompanying Hawk, Emri, and Broken Tooth out onto the frozen expanses in search of game to feed the villagers.

The People of the Deer, fine hunters on their own, had developed a sort of spear that none of the newcomers had ever seen before. The spear points, made out of ivory or stone had been carved with hooked barbs along their sharpened edges. These barbs, once sunk in flesh, remained there, making it almost impossible for the animal to dislodge.

A further important difference was the fact that these spear points were so fashioned that they could detach from the haft itself, yet they were attached by means of a thin length of leather so that neither the haft nor the point was lost. This worked on most game with the exception of the black sea beasts, who were sometimes able to regain the safety of the water, dragging both valuable point and spear haft with them, never to be seen again.

The killing of the three sea beasts and the return of warmer weather had been but a brief moment of hope, as though the Gods were teasing them, for the storms returned in force and wailed around the dwellings, plucking at the doorflaps and pouring down the smoke holes. Cold, hunger, and despair returned once more.

CHAPTER THIRTY-TWO

The trips into the dark ominous ice cavern grew more and more frequent as the villagers prayed for relief from hunger and cold. Three more tiny bodies were buried in the ice and five more old ones gave up their spirits.

Misery lay heavy on the village and even the mountain of ice seemed to grieve, for it groaned and moaned continuously throughout the day and night. Inside the cavern, the sounds were even more pronounced and seemed to penetrate one's very bones, echoing in the head long after they emerged into the light.

These noises terrified Dawn and she implored Emri to leave. But even she was forced to admit that the People of the Deer were too weak to make any sort of a prolonged journey even if the way could be found through the constant storms.

Oddly, once again the weather had turned. Warmth returned even as powerful winds lashed the coast, breaking the ice into huge cakes and flinging it up on the cold shingle, winds too terrible to allow hunting or travel.

And with the advent of warm weather, the ice mountain grew more and more vocal. The people huddled inside their cold dwellings and listened to the moaning, and wondered if the Gods had heard their prayers.

As hope deserted them, more and more villagers followed Taug into the dark tunnel, even those who had seldom gone before, as their neighbors wondered aloud whether their lack of piety were keeping the Gods from answering their prayers. Into the tunnel they went, blowing their whistles, beating their drums, shaking their rattles, singing their chants, and whispering their prayers.

Included in Emri's whispers as they hovered on the edge of the black abyss were prayers of another sort, prayers for a sign that would enable him to speak to Taug about leaving. For it was Emri's intention to leave the village as soon as the storms abated.

As much as he wished it to happen, he also dreaded the moment, for Taug had spent his life in the village, leading his tribe to the best of his ability, and Ermi knew that it would be hard for him to relinquish control.

The trips inside the ice tunnel had become more and more oppressive. As the weather grew warmer and a soft wind blew steadily from the south, wailing around the edges of the mountain, it seemed to grow worse. Emri could all but feel the tension tingling on his skin every time he entered the cavern. It also appeared that the tunnel was moving.

It seemed ridiculous to think that anything as large as the mountain of ice could actually move, but he grew more certain of it with his every pilgrimage.

The moans and groans and sounds of rending deep within the ice terrified him still, but he had ceased mentioning it, for Taug dismissed them with a twitch of his wrinkled hand, replying that it was only their prayers echoing inside the God's ear. Of this, Emri was not so sure, but there seemed little point in arguing, as Taug refused to believe that the sounds signaled danger.

The flow of water had resumed once more and now the bottom of the tunnel ran with a heavy white stream that carved a trench across the beach and entered the waters beyond.

One day, Emri, more certain than ever that the mountain was moving, placed a series of ten small bones upright in the ground at the leading edge of the icy flank, each two paces apart. The next morning, two of them had vanished.

Emri hurried to Taug's dwelling, fear lying heavy on his heart, and blurted out the terrible news.

Taug lifted his white cauled eyes to Emri and then turned aside and huddled further inside his furskins. Washona, wrinkled and thin, her white hair sparse upon her skull, did not even stop what she was doing, but continued rolling a lamp wick out of moss as though he had merely commented on the weather.

"Did you not hear what I said, Father?" asked Emri, fear turning his bones to water, the need to run weighing on him.

"I heard," replied Taug in his small, quavering voice as he stared ahead, blindly. "The Gods wish to be nearer their people. They cannot hear our words and so draw closer. It is a sign. We must cross the chasm and go further, further into the mountain, to find the Gods themselves."

Emri was dumbstruck. How could Taug interpret the signs in this manner? This was no message from the Gods, or if it were, it was no sign from a friendly God, but rather one who wished their deaths.

"But, Taug," Emri began in desperation. But Taug turned his back on Emri and drew his furskins around him until there was nothing to be seen but the crown of his head.

"We will journey into the very heart of the mountain and touch the Gods when the light of the sun shines down on us tomorrow," decreed Taug. "All will go. All. Everyone must go and shake the mountain with the strength of our prayers. Then the Gods will hear us and answer our prayers."

And nothing Emri said would change his mind.

All night long Emri lay awake listening to the sound of the wind screaming around the groaning mountain. It sounded to him like the wail of spirits who had not found their way to the next world, and he feared what was to come with the dawn.

He was wakened by the blowing of whistles. For a moment he lay beneath the heavy bearskin, listening to the eerie dissonance, wondering if it were but a trick of the wind, for the whistles were sounding alarm.

Cold fear shot down Emri's spine and he threw the furskin from him and leaped to his feet, for at that moment he had felt the earth tremble beneath him. His mind raced and he wondered if it were happening, that which he feared most, that the mountain was moving forward at a rapid rate and would crush them all beneath its terrible weight.

He pulled Dawn from her furskin and screamed for Hawk and Mosca, who was grunting and moaning in fear, and together they rushed from the confines of the dwelling.

His first glance was toward the mountain, and he had but a heartbeat to realize that it had not moved before his attention was drawn to the north by some movement or sound. And what he saw was more terrifying than even he would have imagined.

Thundering down on the sleeping village was a herd of massive wooly tuskers, a herd such as they had prayed for all through the long hungry Cold Time. They were wrapped in fog and mist that drifted in from the icy waters, appearing like spirits more imagined than real. But as they reached the first dwelling and smashed it beneath their great feet, the sounds of the rib bones splintering and the shrieks barely begun before they ceased, Emri knew that it was no dream.

"Run! Run!" he yelled, Dawn screaming beside him, Hawk adding his own voice as they watched the tuskers pound through the village—trampling this dwelling, sparing that one—their trunks waving in the air, long coarse hair matted atop the thrashing limbs and swaying bodies.

Emri saw the flash and wild roll of their eyes, smelled the fear-stink of them as they rushed past and vanished into the gloom at the far edge of the village.

It had taken no more than a handful of heartbeats from the first appearance to the last glimpse, yet more than half the village lay in ruins. Dwellings were crushed, those within surely either dead or dying.

Emri stood staring at the devastation before him, wondering if he had failed the people who were to have been his to guide. Wondering if he should have forced Taug to listen, to have moved the people in spite of his objections. And he wondered once again if the Gods were listening to their prayers and if this were their answer.

Dawn was weeping beside him, her face wet with tears, and Hawk cradled her in his arms, while he met Emri's gaze, his own eyes mirroring the fear and awfulness of the situation.

Mosca cowered against Emri's legs, bawling out his own distress. As Emri stepped forward on shaking legs in answer to the first tremulous cries from the shattered village, the cat remained behind, wheeling in first one direction and then another as though seeking a safety that did not exist.

A third of the tribe was dead, killed outright by the huge shaggy beasts, and fully half of those remaining had suffered some injury. Those who had been spared walked among the injured and the dead with glassy eyes, and seemed to take some guilt upon themselves that they too had not been marked.

The dawn rose upon the scene, shining brightly on the ravaged ruins, smoke rising from a few small fires, people sitting on the cold hard ground in silence, their grief and their pain all but overwhelmed by their shock, unable to comprehend what had befallen them and why.

And then, Taug, mercifully spared although Washona had been killed as she slept beside him, lifted his eyes from what little remained of her body and looked upon the mountain.

"Hear, O People of the Deer, the Gods are speaking to us," he said in a loud voice that rang out over the desolate gathering. "The Gods share our grief and call to us to come to them. We must do as they bid. We will enter the mountain and stand at their ear, and they will hear our message and shine upon us once more and we will live in the light of their love."

And to Emri's utter disbelief, here and there, people began to rise, clutching arms, heads, sides, blood still seeping from their wounds, and trailed after Taug as he walked toward the mouth of the cavern with a sure and steady step, the words of their prayers lifting up in solemn reverence.

One after another the people rose and followed him, entering the dark mouth of the tunnel.

Only then did the sounds penetrate Emri's stunned mind. Only then did the loud groans emanating from the mountain of ice sink into his consciousness. Only then did he realize that he had been hearing the sounds for some time now and that they had a tone different from ever before.

It was a deeper sound somehow, one that seemed to issue from the very heart and soul of the mountain, as though it were tearing itself apart in some secret place, at the very center of its being. And Emri knew without a doubt that what he had feared was undoubtedly about to happen; the mountain was on the move.

"Stop, don't go in there!" he cried as he flung himself at the line of villagers who disappeared into the mouth of the cavern one after another. But they did not stop, not even when Emri pointed to the spot where the rib bones had once stood and tried to explain that all of the bones, all, had now vanished.

Men entered, men with whom he had hunted, men with whom he had laughed, men whom he cared about. Women, old, young, mothers, mothers of mothers. Children, some too small to walk and others with the blush of adults on their unformed faces, all passed him by and were swallowed in the maw of the cavern. Fawn Woman, Speaker, Broken Tooth, and Walks Alone, all entered the cavern.

The last of them had gone, and only he and Hawk, Mosca, and Dawn remained on the beach with the dead and the dying.

"I have to get them back! They must leave or they'll die!" he cried, shaking with fear and wanting to run but knowing that he could not.

Hawk came to his side and made as if to enter, but Dawn flung herself at them both, crying and screaming, "No! No! No!" over and over. Mosca began to bawl and cower against the sand, his eyes wild in his head.

"Take her," Emri said, grabbing Dawn and placing her firmly in Hawk's arms. "Take Mosca. Cross the ice to the other side and wait for me. I will be back, I promise." With one last glimpse at the sky above, he too turned and plunged into the darkness of the cave and was gone.

CHAPTER THIRTY-THREE

Sound was all around him. The mountain seemed alive, groaning and moaning as though in mortal pain. Even worse were the deep, rending sounds like flesh being torn in two.

The flow of water had become a rushing torrent, pouring down the floor of the tunnel, filling it from side to side, sloshing over the top of Emri's boots and numbing his feet.

Instead of the total darkness that he was accustomed to, the tunnel was now lit by an eerie gloom that did nothing to reassure him. It was obvious that fissures were opening above the tunnel, allowing light to enter. If they opened further, as surely they must do in the warmth of the sun, the tunnel would collapse.

His fear drove him on at a reckless pace and soon he caught up with the last of the line of villagers. Icy water dribbled down on them from the ceiling, plastering their hair to their heads.

"Go back! Go back!" Emri implored, his words echoing wildly in the tunnel. He took a stunned woman by the arm, turned her around forcibly and shoved her toward the entrance.

"Go back!" he cried, shaking a man by the shoulders as he attempted to push past. Some listened to him, others did not. Some few merely required a word to release them from the terrible command. Others would not listen at all and looked at him with glassy eyes, and continued on into the heart of the mountain.

Emri could feel a constant tremor in the ice beneath his feet and in the walls themselves whenever he reached out to steady himself. He knew without a doubt that the tunnel was about to collapse.

Everything in him screamed for escape; his legs longed to run back toward the far-distant circle of light that signified safety, but he could not allow himself to do so while it was still possible to save the others.

Before him, the darkness closed in again, the light dimming to a murky gloom. As though to further complicate matters, a thick fog had begun to rise from the water at his feet, filling the cavern with trailing shadows and misty images.

He began to hear the *chink, chink, chink* of ice falling, but to his mind, it sounded like softly shaking rattles. The steady tremor beneath his feet became the beat of a giant drum. He heard the mountain's groans and it became the people's chants. He smelled incense where none should be, and he was afraid.

And then they were there before him, the last of the People of the Deer; those who followed Taug through loyalty or through fear. They were ahead of him, wrapped in the wraithlike mist, hovering on the edge of the abyss, seeking a way across.

The mountain had begun to groan even more loudly, and suddenly the ground shifted beneath Emri's feet, throwing him to his knees. He heard the people scream in fear, and Taug's voice lifted above the deep, sounds of the earth in anguish.

"Do not fear," he cried, his voice strong and triumphant. "We are almost there. The Gods are close-by us and await our prayers. We must go to them now!"

Emri flung himself forward, clawing his way through the crowd, shoving them back behind him, hoping they would leave while they were still able.

"*No!*" he cried forcefully. "Do not go further, or you will die. It is not the Gods who call to you but death! There are no Gods here. The mountain is dying and you will die too unless you leave. You must go now!"

And then it happened. As Taug's voice lifted up in bold, ecstatic tones, chanting prayers to his Gods, the mountain shuddered; and with a deep tearing sound, the ground sagged beneath them. Chunks of the roof began to fall, pelting them with ice, some pieces as small as hail, others much larger. One such piece struck Emri on the side of his head, driving him to his knees, his vision spinning dizzily.

Screams of terror echoed throughout the tunnel and then a shaft of light appeared above them, blinding in its intensity though filtered through many layers of ice.

The moisture-laden air swirled with mist and a great stag emerged from the heart of the fog, its pelt and wide-spread rack beaded with moisture. It looked at Emri, its clear brown eyes attempting to dominate, commanding, demanding his fealty.

"We are the People of the Deer," it thundered, its voice becoming one with the deep, rumbling groans that filled the cavern. And it seemed to Emri that he could hear the same eerie whistles that had accompanied the stag during its first manifestation and the scent of incense was thick in his nostrils.

As he struggled to clear his head and gain his footing on the shaking ground, his arm was gripped in a tight embrace. Emri tried to pull free, terrified that it was Taug who gripped him and would take him to his death.

But a voice called his name and he looked up and saw that it was Broken Tooth, his face pale and eyes clear. "We've got to get out!" cried Broken Tooth. "The whole mountain is breaking up!"

Emri nodded his agreement, and, with Broken Tooth's help, crawled to his feet and began edging his way back along the quivering wall, looking away from the figure of the stag. God it well might be, but if so, it was the God of death, not of life.

"Come!" said the stag. "Come unto the Gods!" And so commanding was its tone that Emri found himself turning back in spite of himself.

As he watched, spellbound, the stag leaped, its powerful body straining forward, hooves reaching for the far side, attempting to span the broad abyss. And then it disappeared from sight.

One after the other, as though still listening to some inner voice, the people began to gather at the edge of the awful darkness, gathering their courage to follow where the stag had led, going to meet their God.

"*No!*" screamed Emri, flinging himself forward only to be jerked back by Broken Tooth. He watched in horror as, one after the other, the people stepped into darkness.

There was a moment when Fawn Woman stepped forward and Walks Alone appeared at her side. He looked at Emri, his dark eyes full of the tumult of emotion and unspoken words as he reached out for Fawn Woman, and then they were gone. Forever after, Emri was uncertain whether Walks Alone had been trying to hold her back or keep her beside him, even in the world beyond.

He was brought back to the present by an even more ominous shift in the ground, and with a thunderous roar the ceiling collapsed above and beyond the abyss, burying those who had followed their God, cutting them off forever from those who had remained behind.

There were no whistles, no chants, no drums, no rattles, and no incense on the way back, only blind terror as those who were left scrambled through the dark quaking tunnel, dodging falls of ice and crumbling walls.

They poured out of the mouth of the tunnel and ran across the beach, noticing as they ran that there was now only a short distance between the mountain of ice and the water's edge. The mountain was on the move.

Urged on by their own terror and the screams of those who had gathered on the far edge of the ice lobe, they raced for safety.

All but two had succeeded in grasping the outstretched hands that reached for them as the mountain of ice collapsed with a rumble that shook the ground.

Everyone, those who had emerged from the tunnel and those who waited, were flung through the air, slammed forward as though by a giant unseen fist by the tremendous wave of air displaced by the collapsing glacier.

The two who had not reached safety were buried beneath the immense wall of ice that had broken from the mountain and stretched far, far out into the water. Of the tunnel and those who had gone into the abyss, there was no sign.

There were no more of them than could be numbered on the fingers of five hands. There were women and children and men, often not belonging to each other. But their mothers, fathers, mates, and loved ones lay dead beneath the ice. Those who remained would form new families and new bonds in order to endure.

They had no weapons, no food, no tools, and no clothes other than those they wore, but they had courage and inner strength, and they would survive.

ABOUT THE AUTHOR

Rose Estes has lived at various times in her life in Chicago, Houston, Mexico, Canada, a driftwood house on an island, a log cabin in the mountains, and a broken Volkswagen van.

She presently shares her life with an eccentric game designer/cartoonist, three children, one slightly demented dog, and a pride of cats.

While it is true that she did not live in a cave and eat roots and berries while writing this series, a great deal of research has gone into its making.

Ms. Estes lists reading, movies, animals, kids, tropical rain forests, and good coffee as the things that make her most happy.

She currently makes her home in Lake Geneva, Wisconsin, where she is working on the next volume in the SAGA OF THE LOST LANDS.

Coming in September

SAGA OF THE LOST LANDS

Volume Three:
Spirit of The Hawk

by
Rose Estes

The exciting conclusion
to the adventures begun in

Blood of the Tiger
and
Brother to the Lion

Follow Emri and Hawk as they struggle
for survival and surpremacy in a savage
prehistoric world.